EPHRAIM
A Rabbi Strays...

A NOVEL

SAM GOLDENBERG

To Rosi,
My loving wife & greatest fan — a Happy Birthday.
Sam

Copyright © 2014 by Sam Goldenberg
First Edition – June 2014

ISBN
978-1-4602-4291-9 (Hardcover)
978-1-4602-4292-6 (Paperback)
978-1-4602-4293-3 (eBook)

All rights reserved.

No part of this publication may be reproduced in any form, or by any means, electronic or mechanical, including photocopying, recording, or any information browsing, storage, or retrieval system, without permission in writing from the publisher.

Produced by:

FriesenPress
Suite 300 – 852 Fort Street
Victoria, BC, Canada V8W 1H8

www.friesenpress.com

Distributed to the trade by The Ingram Book Company

Table of Contents

PROLOGUE: Elijah the Prophet i

CHAPTER 1: Homecoming 1

CHAPTER 2: A Dilemma 14

CHAPTER 3: Rabbis Without Borders 28

CHAPTER 4: At The Brink 43

CHAPTER 5: Elijah Is Not Happy 57

CHAPTER 6: The Rabbi Makes A Decision 69

CHAPTER 7: The Rabbi Lays Out A Strategy 81

CHAPTER 8: The Enemy Strikes 89

CHAPTER 9: The Family Is Not Happy 102

CHAPTER 10: The Enemy Strikes Again 114

CHAPTER 11: Travels In Ancient Egypt 126

CHAPTER 12: The Woman Of Nahel Sorek 137

CHAPTER 13: Decisions, Decisions 151

CHAPTER 14: The Rabbi Decides 156

GLOSSARY OF : Jewish Terms 164

About the Author 167

Acknowledgements 168

Dedicated to Rosemarie, my wife of many years,
for her encouragement and support.

PROLOGUE

Elijah the Prophet

Whenever Ephraim encountered truly stressful moments, Elijah the Prophet visited in the privacy of his bedroom at night. The first time this occurred, Ephraim was in his early teens, wrestling with his conscience and the joys of awakening sexuality.

Ephraim knew it was Elijah the moment he appeared. The prophet was imposing —tall, draped in a long flowing red robe that engulfed his body, a voluminous grey-white beard framing a gaunt face with a thin nose surmounted by deep-set brown eyes and a lined forehead.

I'm having a dream, Ephraim thought.

"Of course," the Prophet agreed. "I appear only in dreams. Nevertheless, I am an old man and would be grateful to be seated."

Ephraim leapt from the bed and pulled a chair out from his desk. The Prophet sat down with a sigh of relief.

"Thank you. Now for what is bothering you. Like all maturing young Israelites, you must learn to control your primal impulses. There is no compromise, no easy way."

Ephraim fell into a deep sleep and when he awoke in the morning, Elijah was gone and the chair was at his desk.

That first time was over ten years ago.

There were many visits after that. Once he was angry with his father for insisting he complete his homework before watching his favourite TV program. Elijah was not sympathetic.

"How dare you think ill of your father," the Prophet roared. "Is it not clearly stated in the Torah that you must love and respect your father and mother?" The next morning, Ephraim apologized to his father and was rewarded with a hug and a kiss.

He was visited by Elijah the night he lost his virginity at a wild university frat party. At home later, Ephraim lay in bed, suffering pangs of fear and regret. What if the girl became pregnant? What if he contracted a deadly sexual disease?

"Foolish boy," Elijah laughed disdainfully. "The time to worry about consequences is before the act. Sow your seed in the garden of Israel, not in the desert's barren wastes. Choose wisely."

Now 27 years old, Ephraim saw the golden haze descend into his room and once again, Elijah stood before him. He jumped off the bed and pulled out the chair.

"You are very perturbed and your problem seems to be a person. Tell me what is bothering you."

"Prophet Elijah, it is very difficult. It may take a while."

"Time is of consequence to you, but not to me. Speak."

Hesitantly, Ephraim began, "The problem started after I was confirmed as a rabbi and returned home..."

CHAPTER 1

Homecoming

Just after noon in early May of 2007, Ephraim Zimmerman walked through the US Arrivals gate at Toronto's Pearson International Airport and into the welcoming arms of his mother. Marsha's tears ran freely as she embraced her son.

"My Freml!" she exclaimed happily, using his Yiddish nickname. "A Rabbi! Did they give you a certificate? Everybody must see your certificate."

Tall and muscular, he laughed as he clasped his arms around his mother and lifted her off the ground. "I hope you've arranged an open car parade down Bathurst Street."

His own eyes filled with tears as he contemplated his mother. He had missed her. In the four years at New York's Yeshiva University, he had come home once two years ago for his father's funeral. During the summer sessions and the High Holidays, he'd been posted to congregations in small towns in New Jersey and Virginia for practical experience. His contact with home had been frequent phone calls.

As usual, his mother was well turned out in a grey suit and black low-heeled shoes, coiffed hair highlighting a remarkably unlined and attractive face.

Marsha stepped back and inspected him. "Very nice," she said. "The blue pin-stripe fits you well."

He wore the usual fedora but was unbearded, preferring instead sideburns that crept just below the cheek bones. He had the long Zimmerman face with the square jaw, prominent nose and thoughtful blue eyes.

"You're such a good-looking young man," Marsha said. "You'll have no trouble finding a wife."

He laughed. "Right now, all I want to find is a job."

He wrestled his huge suitcase into the trunk of the Cadillac sedan and sat in the passenger seat beside his mother.

"I didn't think you'd come to the airport. Who's minding the shop or did you close it for a while?"

She owned a gift shop, a legacy of his father, in the Esplanade, a large mall on Bathurst Street, a few blocks north of Steeles Avenue in uptown Toronto. Ephraim had worked in the shop during his high school years.

"No, you can't close during mall hours. They fine you. I'm very lucky. Three months ago, I hired a young girl, a shiksa, to help me in the store. She's turned out to be a real find. I left her in charge for the rest of the afternoon."

Ephraim frowned. "You're satisfied she's honest? Ma, retail is such a cash business."

Marsha was silent as she steered the car onto the 401, the highway that cuts across the middle of Toronto, selected the East exit ramp, swept past a truck and settled into the slow lane. "It's not the first time I've left her alone and I never found any money missing. She's a nice young woman and I can tell, she's well brought up. You don't have to worry. And besides, as a rabbi, I thought you're supposed to trust people."

He reached over and stroked her cheek. "I trust you, Ma, and others as I get to know them. New York didn't improve my trust factor. I didn't want to worry you so I never told you about my experiences as a resident of the Bronx. I often heard gun shots and one of my friends was mugged and killed as he bicycled home one night. Even Adam couldn't be trusted. Or Samson. The Bible is full of our heroes who couldn't follow the Almighty's simple commands."

She laughed as she guided the car around an emergency vehicle with its red and yellow lights blinking. "It's not Shabbat and already I'm getting a sermon."

Grinning, he leaned back in his seat. He'd forgotten his mother's wry sense of humour, her ability to poke gentle fun at him. When he'd returned for the few weeks when his father died, there had been no jokes, no laughter, just the grief attending the sudden, unforeseen death of a beloved husband and father.

For a few days, he had considered giving up his studies and returning home to help his mother. "Absolutely not," she told him. "I can run the store. Your career is more important. Your daddy was so proud you were studying to be a rabbi. If you stop now, you will cause him pain in Heaven." Ephraim wasn't sure her theology was right but he went back to New York.

EPHRAIM

There was a lapse in conversation as Marsha focussed her attention on the highway's heavy traffic.

"How are you doing, Ma?" Ephraim asked. "It's two years since daddy died. Are there men in your life?"

"Your uncle Avram," Marsha said, "has made a proposal. He says, according to Jewish law, it's the duty of a brother to marry the brother's widow."

Ephraim nodded, frowning. "Well, that's an ancient tradition. Are you interested?"

The car swerved threateningly as she snapped her head around. "Absolutely not! I'm fifty-five and he's seventy and not in the best health. He doesn't want a wife — he wants a nurse."

Poor uncle Avram, Ephraim thought, he probably loves my mother. She turned north onto the Allen Expressway, concentrating on the circular curve that led up to the roadway. "As for other men, within weeks of your daddy's passing away, the phone calls began. 'Just thought we might have a coffee some day' was the usual line. I told them I was in mourning for the full year. As soon as the year was over, the phone began ringing again. Freml, they're all old men. One's in his eighty's. I still have lots of life left in me. Now that you're home, maybe you'll screen my calls for me."

"Ma, I'm a rabbi, not a matchmaker. But I'll do what I can to help you."

The family home was a large condominium on the tenth floor of a high rise building just off Steeles Avenue near Bathurst Street. His room was exactly as he had left it. Windows filled the south wall and gave a panoramic view of downtown Toronto and its skyscraper profile, punctuated by the CN Tower like an exclamation mark.

"Now that you're a rabbi," his mother said, "you can change what you have hanging on the walls."

His room was festooned with pennants and posters from his favourite teams, the Toronto Maple Leafs and the Blue Jays.

He shook his head. "No, Ma. Maybe my prayers will rub off. The teams need all the help they can get."

He was still unpacking when the doorbell buzzed. A few moments elapsed and then it buzzed again.

"Freml, dear, can you let your Uncle Avram in. He's stuck in the lobby vestibule. He can't seem to figure out how to get from the bell to the door in time to open it."

His uncle was all smiles as Ephraim opened the lobby door. A typical Zimmerman, he was tall, a little bent now, leaning on a cane, thin, almost gaunt except for the waistline bulge. The usual long Zimmerman face had thinned even more and hollow cheeks emphasized the prominent nose. A few wisps of white hair still clung to the top of his head. The round eyes, bright and cheerful, beamed out at Ephraim its message of welcome and admiration.

"Our Freml a rabbi!" Uncle Avram exclaimed. "Mazeltov! If only your father — may he rest in peace — could have waited." They embraced.

As they entered the elevator, his uncle stopped on the threshold and turned. "Do you have a shul yet?"

Ephraim gently pushed his uncle on to the elevator as the door closed. "No, not yet. I'm trying to decide where I want to serve."

"Serve? That's what you do in a restaurant. A rabbi needs a shul, a congregation. Even in Toronto, we need more rabbis."

Ephraim grinned but said nothing. He hadn't told his mother what he had in mind.

Uncle Avram greeted Marsha warmly and tried to kiss her but she held him off.

"Avram, I've made a little snack for Ephraim. Will you have some?"

They sat around the table in the bow window eating area off the large kitchen. It was already three o'clock and the snack consisted of tea and cinnamon coffee cake.

"You know what else you need?" Avram said, munching on cake. "You need a wife, a rebbetsyn, who will help you and give your mother some grandchildren."

"Avram, leave him alone." Marsha poured her son another cup of tea and pushed the milk and sugar bowls towards him. "He'll find a wife when he's ready. Besides, he just got home. I want to look after him for a little while."

"Marsha, when will you have time to look after him? You're always busy with the store. And I've got just the girl for him. One of Gertie's piano students is a nice girl from a family I know well — Zifkin — and she just turned twenty-five. Freml has to meet her and Gertie said she can arrange it."

Marsha was indignant. "Avram, he's hardly home ten minutes and already you've got him walking down the aisle." Whatever else she was going to say was interrupted by loud knocking at the apartment door.

"Hi, Mrs. Zimmermann," Alex Feldman greeted Marsha with a flying kiss as he breezed past her. "Just came to say hello to Freml."

Ephraim jumped up, delighted to see his best friend. Alex was short and stocky, a shock of unruly brown hair crowned a round smiling face with bright, mischievous blue eyes.

"Well, this is a happier time since we last saw each other," Alex said. "You're now a rabbi. Mazeltov. I guess that means the good times we had are over."

"That's right," Uncle Avram said. "He cannot join you in your sinful ways. Last Sunday I saw you walking through the Esplanade with a girl on each arm."

Alex grinned. "That just shows I'm ambidextrous."

"How're you doing otherwise?" Ephraim asked, as he pulled out a chair for Alex.

Alex helped himself to cake. "I'm doing very well, knock wood." — tapping his head — "I've been involved in all the M&A work that's going on and I'm only a year into the job. A couple more years and I can buy my first Ferrari."

"When you do, I want a ride," Ephraim said.

"I'm coming too," Marsha added.

Uncle Avram looked worried. "Don't encourage him. He is the evil eye sent by the Almighty to tempt Freml."

"Oh, Avram. Don't be so ridiculous. And since when is a ride in a car temptation? My Freml will be too busy with his work, anyway." She turned to Ephraim. "What are your plans now that you're graduated?"

Ephraim was silent for a moment. "I'm not sure. I have an appointment to see Rabbi Sholom Nitsky on Monday morning at the Chevra Kadisha Institute."

Uncle Avram put down his cup. "But the Chevra Kadisha sends rabbis all over the world. Who knows where you'll end up?"

"Mr. Zimmerman," Alex said, "they send rabbis where they're needed. They're not needed in Toronto. Good for you, Freml. I just couldn't see you following the conventional path."

Marsha had tears in her eyes. "Freml, sweetheart, I can't bear the thought of you not being here."

Ephraim put an arm around his mother's shoulders. "Ma, I won't be far away. I've already corresponded with the Institute and, if they hire me, my first assignment is probably Nova Scotia, not Halifax but all the small towns where there are only a few Jews left. I'll be an itinerant rabbi. It's a tremendous learning opportunity and I'd like to do it for a few years. If I stay in Toronto, I'll be the sub-sub-rabbi in a large shul. At any rate, I'll be here all summer."

His mother smiled bravely through her tears. "Freml, I'm sure you've thought it through and it's all for the best."

"How is it for the best?" Uncle Avram demanded. "How will he find a nice Jewish girl in Nova Scotia? They've all moved here. Besides, what girl will marry a man without a fixed address? What is with this younger generation? Even the young rabbis are mishuga."

His uncle had stood up. Ephraim reached out and grasped a flailing arm. "Uncle Avram, it's not good for you to get excited. I really don't intend to settle down for a few years and I'm not looking for a wife. But if it makes you feel better, Gertie can introduce me to her student. But that's all it is — an introduction. If I wanted an arranged marriage, I had many opportunities in New York. My teachers were eager to get rid of their daughters."

"And why not?" Marsha said, stroking Ephraim's cheek. "Such a smart, handsome boy."

"If you're looking for women in Halifax," Alex offered, a broad grin lighting up his face, "I have some addresses."

Avram wagged a finger at Alex. "He doesn't need your addresses."

"Oh calm down, Avram. Alex is just teasing. Freml, why don't you tell us about New York?"

During the remainder of the afternoon, he told them about his experiences in the city and at the university. The discussion broke up when Ephraim left for the evening prayers.

"I'll drive you over to the Clark Street shul," Marsha suggested. "I have to go to the store and see how my girl is making out. Why don't you come over after the service and we'll go home together?" The Clark Synagogue was only a ten minute walk from the Esplanade.

It was almost closing time for the mall when he arrived at the store. It was warm and he had removed his hat, his head partially covered by a black skullcap. Marsha was about to lock the door. "Come in and wait while we close down and balance. This is Laura Burton who I couldn't do without."

Ephraim nodded to the woman busily counting the cash behind the counter. She barely acknowledged him but continued working away with Marsha helping. Finally, Laura came around the counter and smiling, held out a hand to Ephraim. "I'm sorry to have appeared rude but if I lost my count I'd have to start over. I've never met a rabbi before. Your mother says you've just graduated and you came first in your class. Congratulations." They shook hands.

He guessed she was the same age as he, average height, an attractive figure, a pretty face with her lips slightly puckered, a pert nose, large grey-green eyes, and straight brown hair that scraped her shoulders. He felt an instant liking for her and put it down to her forthright, chatty manner — clearly a good salesperson.

"Thank you," he said, blushing. "All sons come first in their class. My mother tells me you're a great help to her and I'm grateful to you for that."

Laura smiled at Marsha. "I've warned her she's training her competition. I've learned more from your mother in three months than I learned from my retailing course in two years. Someday, I shall open my own shop. I don't know whether I'll stick with gifts. I'm very fond of shoes — perhaps it'll be a shoe store."

Marsha was turning off lights. "Whatever you decide, I'm sure you'll do well. But now it's time to go. Laura, do you need a lift?"

"No, thanks Mrs. Zimmerman. My boyfriend's waiting outside."

The next few days, Ephraim was busy visiting relatives and receiving their congratulations. Uncle Avram appointed himself tour director and drove Ephraim to the various locations. Avram's daughter Gertie gave him an impromptu concert in her living room by three of her students — two teenage boys and a young woman.

"You must meet my star pupil," Gertie said, pulling the young woman forward after the two boys had left. "This is Rebecca Zifkin."

Wow, thought Ephraim, Uncle Avram sure knows how to pick 'em. Rebecca was tall and slender, dressed in a T-shirt and tight fitting jeans that emphasized an alluring bosom, narrow waist, and trim buttocks. Sparkling blue eyes, long blonde hair tied in a pony tail, and full sensuous lips completed the picture.

"Are you planning to be a pianist?" Ephraim asked.

Rebecca laughed. "No, I'm really not that good, despite what Gertie says. I'm a parochial school teacher and I'd like to be able to play Yiddish folk songs and Klezmer music."

Gertie insisted they had to have tea and Rebecca must join them.

"Let me help you," Rebecca said and followed Gertie into the kitchen.

"What do you think?" Avram asked. "Was I wrong?"

"She's very pretty, no doubt about that. I'm sure she's a nice woman. But like I said, I have to get my feet on the ground, get some work experience before I can think of marrying."

Avram shrugged his shoulders and rolled his eyes skyward. "Vai, Vai, Vai! By the time you get around to it, she'll be gone. The vultures are circling. The girl has money. Why should the money go to some stranger?"

Money was an obsession with his uncle. His entire working life had been a succession of hapless enterprises. He had started off in the needle trade, opening a factory specializing in vests. For several years the enterprise was profitable, then vests went out of style. At one point, he decided the car business was the place to be. He bought a filling station on a busy street, and, ahead of his time, added a small shop for snacks and drinks. A year later, the street was closed to through traffic to make way for an overhead bridge structure. His last foray into the business world was to scrape his savings together and invest in a dot.com file sharing venture run by a "completely trustworthy son of an old friend." When the tech bubble burst, the business collapsed, along with Avram's investment. Retired now, he lived on his government pensions and regular contributions from his more successful brothers and sisters.

"Besides," Uncle Avram continued, "you're in the same line of work."

Rebecca returned with platters of party sandwiches and pastries. "Gertie wants me to assure you that everything is kosher."

Ephraim nodded. "I never doubted it. Tell me, what sparked your interest in teaching at parochial schools?"

She leaned forward in the sofa chair. "It's an interest in all things Jewish. I believe Jewish boys and girls should know about their traditions and about their culture that is slowly disappearing. Everybody thinks that because there's a State of Israel, Judaism is safe. But Israel is mostly secular and in the Diaspora, the secular trend is very strong. I'd like to help fight this trend. I plan someday to open my own school."

Ephraim looked at her, his eyes wide in admiration. She spoke with such fervour and independence that he wondered what sort of rabbi's wife she would make. He couldn't see her meekly adapting to the orthodox tradition — his helpmate, subservient to his wishes, mistress of his home, responsible to bear and raise the children. Yet he fancied the fire in her.

"Why did you become a rabbi?" Rebecca asked.

He pondered the question for a long moment. The silence became embarrassing. Rebecca sat back and crossed her legs. Uncle Avram looked at him, his eyebrows raised questioningly. Gertie came in then with pots of coffee and tea. "Please help yourselves."

They filled their plates with sandwiches and pastries while Gertie poured the tea or coffee.

"You haven't answered my question," Rebecca reminded him.

"I find it difficult to answer." He paused, sipped his coffee and took a bite out of a sandwich. "As a teenager, I wasn't particularly religious. When I graduated from high school, I was at a loss what to do next. My friend Alex Feldman convinced me I should join him in getting a business degree. I took a year at U of T but I wasn't happy. My life seemed empty, lacking purpose."

He stared out the window, oblivious of his audience.. "During my year at U of T, I sat in on a Bible study class which translated the Hebrew into English. I got hooked. It wasn't just the stories — we all know the stories. It was the language, the grandeur of the classical Hebrew that captured me. I wanted to learn more. That's why I went to Yeshiva U. I thought I would try it for a year and four years later I'm a rabbi."

"Are you telling us you became a rabbi by accident?" Gertie asked.

Uncle Avram was shaking his head and muttering, "This young generation — they're all mishuga."

Ephraim shook his head. "Not exactly by accident. All I'm saying is I didn't set out with a goal to become a rabbi."

"OK," Rebecca said. "Now you're a rabbi. Are you convinced you made the right choice?"

"Time will tell. I need to work at it for a while — to see that being a rabbi accomplishes something."

Rebecca leaned towards him, grasping her knees with both hands. "Rabbi means leader, guide, teacher. Surely the opportunity to lead a flock of your people in support of their religious and cultural needs will give you a sense of satisfaction. We are like soldiers in the same fight — to bolster our heritage, I as a teacher, you as a rabbi."

Ephraim was taken aback by her intensity and paused before responding. "This may sound very strange. I don't see myself in a battle against secularism. Of course I believe in our religion and will strongly support it. But there are many individuals for whom observing all the rules is just not on. What am I to do? Ignore them? I'd rather work with them. Take my friend Alex Feldman. I'm sure he hasn't seen the inside of a synagogue since his Bar-Mitzvah. If I start preaching to him, I'll lose him as a friend and his friendship is very valuable to me."

"Humph!" Rebecca exclaimed. "I know Alex Feldman. He's a Jew in name only. All he cares about is business and having a good time. He's the type who'd think nothing about intermarrying — that's if he ever decides to marry. By the way, would you marry a Jew and a Gentile?"

He shrugged his shoulders. "As a rabbi, I'm supposed to say 'no.' I think I'd look at the situation before deciding."

She stood up, thrusting her fists forward. "Under what circumstances can a rabbi marry a Jew and a Gentile?"

For a moment, he basked in the warmth of her fiery indignation. "Suppose I felt that the two people were deeply in love, truly committed to each other whether a ceremony took place or not, then I could conclude that marriage was the right thing. I would spend my energy trying to convince the gentile to convert or to persuade them that the children should be raised as Jews."

"Well, now I've heard everything." She looked at her watch. "Sorry but I've got to go. I promised my parents I'd be home in time for dinner."

She thanked Gertie for the refreshments, mumbled "Nice to have met you" to Ephraim and marched out of the house.

Uncle Avram's face looked even more sallow and gaunt as he voiced his despair. "There's one bride you can cross off your list."

Gertie laughed. "Papa, don't be so negative. She likes him. I'm a woman. I can tell."

He was analyzing his own feelings for Rebecca as he walked slowly along Bathurst Street to a kosher restaurant just south of Steeles Avenue. Marsha was working late that night and he hadn't felt like cooking. Rebecca, he thought, would be easy to fall in love with — a gorgeous face and figure and an exciting, spirited temperament. She was like Rivke — the Rebecca of the Bible — forceful, determined to get her own way. Could he contend with her strength? Would she understand and accept their differences in point of view or would she simply sweep his away? Perhaps it was useless to worry about it. He did not want to even consider marrying now and she was clearly disappointed in him.

A line of joggers ran towards him and he stepped to one side to let them pass. One of the runners waved at him as she ran past and he caught a glimpse of a smiling face, a heaving bosom and shapely buttocks and legs.

Laura Burton's beauty had not gone unnoticed when they first met. He watched her retreating form. His teachers had told him that the best way to quell lust was to meditate on a passage from the Holy Scriptures. He tried but the only text that popped into his mind was from Solomon's Shir ha-Shirim — the Song of Songs:

How beautiful are thy steps in sandals… The roundings of thy thighs… Thy two breasts are like twin fawns… How fair and how pleasant art thou, O love, for delights!

Ridiculous, he thought. Laura Burton is forbidden territory, out of bounds. A lone runner, well behind the pack, stopped in front of him.

"You're not supposed to look at shiksas," a mocking voice said accusingly. Alex Feldman reached out his two arms and grasped Ephraim's shoulders. "Let me hang on a moment or I'll collapse."

Ephraim laughed. "You're going athletic on us. That's not what I remember from our school days. The only running you did then was after girls."

"Well, I'm still running after girls. Most of the other runners are women and I can't keep up. Where are you off to?"

"I was on my way to Ernie's Glatt Kosher for a bite."

Alex looked along the street but the running group was out of sight. "I'll join you but you'll have to pay — I left my wallet in my locker at the Running Club."

"Won't they wonder what happened to you?"

"No, they'll think I died. Another block and I would've died. I need to get back before they close at nine."

Ephraim was happy for the company. They walked along, recalling old times. Ephraim's cell phone rang, Rebecca was on the line.

"I hope you don't mind but Gertie gave me your number. I think I left you with the impression that I was angry but I'm not. I'd like to continue our discussion." They arranged to get together for coffee at the Esplanade on Sunday afternoon.

Alex had caught snippets of the conversation. "I'd recognize that voice anywhere. I'm impressed. You've already met Take-no-prisoners Zifkin. Watch out — she's one beautiful woman but it's my way or the highway."

Ephraim held open the door to the restaurant. "She doesn't like you either," he said, smiling.

They settled at a table and consulted the menus. "We'll have to select dairy or meat dishes — we can't have both on the table."

"Wow, you're a real stickler for the rules."

Ephraim shook his head. "They're not just my rules — they're the restaurant's rules."

They picked cheese blintzes with sour cream, fresh rye bread, and a salad, to be washed down with coffee. The food arrived quickly.

Alex wiped the sweat off his face with a napkin. "She doesn't like me because I admitted that I sometimes dated non-Jewish girls. She also has no sense of humour. I told her one of my projects as a Mergers and Acquisition specialist was acting as an advisor to the Vatican and we were planning to put in a bid for the Wailing Wall. 'If they ever try,' she said, 'the whole Jewish population would rise up.'"

Ephraim made the customary blessing over the bread and they began eating. "You're making fun of the woman my family wants me to marry. If it comes about, you'd be my Best Man at the wedding and you'd have to say something nice."

Alex sat up straight, looked up at the ceiling and raised his right hand in a declamatory gesture. "'Ladies and Gentlemen, tonight we celebrate the joining together in holy matrimony of Rebecca Zifkin — a bride of dazzling beauty and determined views —and Rabbi Ephraim Zimmerman — her soon to be oppressed victim.' Really Freml, I know she's tempting but you better make sure you're with her all the way."

"Alex, why wouldn't I be with her all the way? I'm a rabbi now. I've cast my lot on the side of Judaism. I could easily see us as a husband and wife team running our own school or partnered in some other effort."

Alex buttered a slice of rye bread and chewed away at it. "Freml, I know you. Sure, the two of you could work together, et cetera. But if two gays showed up on your doorstep asking to be married and you felt it was right, you'd marry them even if the next day you were kicked out of the rabbinate. Well, she made it clear to me that homosexuality was a sin, period, full stop. And don't get her on the subject of intermarriage. No, Freml, my guess is, you'd come apart at some time."

"Alex, let's not worry about it. Right now, I just want to get into my work. The last thing I need is to be tied down with marrying or even courting."

Alex stuffed a piece of cheese blintz into his mouth and grinned. "You were looking with great interest after the runners. Which one was it?"

"I know one of them — Laura Burton. She works for my mother." Ephraim had finished eating and was sitting back, enjoying the last dregs of his coffee..

"Laura? Yeah, she is pretty. I was thinking of asking her out until I got a look at her boyfriend. Big guy, bigger than you. Looks ok, but there's something suspicious about him. When you sit down to do an M&A deal, you kind of size up the people at the table. I would worry about him. She hasn't chosen wisely."

"And there's cool, M&A specialist, debonair man about town, Alex Feldman, left out in the cold. I could make a prayer on your behalf."

Alex was chewing away on salad. "Don't bother," he said between swallows. "God's too busy for such trivia. Besides, it might backfire. Did you hear the one about the lemele who, distressed that he's turning fifty and still not married, asks God to make him irresistible to women. There's a puff of smoke and he's turned into a platinum credit card."

Ephraim thumped the table and laughed heartily. "I'll use that in my first sermon."

"Anyway," said Alex, "as a rabbi, you must think differently but I just don't believe in a personal god who worries about little me."

Ephraim was silent for a moment. "I must confess that I range from absolute conviction to worrisome doubts. Yet there must be something that created the universe and guided its development."

Alex shook his head in mock wonderment. "Fantastic! A rabbi with doubts. Well, I have none. The Almighty may have created the universe but the last time we heard from him was 13.75 billion years ago."

Ephraim shrugged his shoulders and downed the last of the coffee. "Big Bang theory. The rest is random chance. I just can't accept that. Even Einstein believed God doesn't play dice."

Ephraim paid the bill. They walked slowly up Bathurst Street. "We'll have to continue our discussion another time, Alex. It's time for Maariv."

"And I better recover my clothes and tell the Running Club I survived the latest ordeal."

CHAPTER 2

A Dilemma

The next day after the morning service, he shopped for a few items his mother had requested at the Clark St. Solly's, a large grocery store, devoted to kosher foods and supervised by a rabbi. He emerged from the store carrying two heavy shopping bags and started back along Clark Street. A voice hailed him and he turned and stared into the smiling face of Laura Burton.

"I come along here every morning on my way to work. I live on Hilda. I saw you the other morning coming out of the synagogue but you were busy talking to some men. May I help you?"

"These bags are awfully heavy. The list my mother gave me was much smaller but I added to it — lots of soul food, at least for me."

She took one bag from him and nearly dropped it. "You're not kidding," she laughed. "But I'm a very strong girl. You saw me running and I also do weights. I want to stay in shape."

He smiled and looked at her. "You're obviously succeeding." She was wearing a white blouse, tucked into a fitted black skirt, emphasizing her trim figure and bosom.

She was clearly pleased with his flattery but changed the subject. "It's rather warm today. Do you always have to wear a hat?"

He removed the hat, revealing a black skullcap underneath. "Our head has to be covered in recognition of the One above."

There was no mistaking the look of admiration as she gazed up at him. "With your hat off, you don't look so serious. You know, based on what your mother has explained to me, yours sounds like a much tougher religion than mine."

They stopped at Bathurst Street, waiting for the light to change. "What is your religion?" he asked.

"I'm Catholic. Not a very good Catholic. I don't go to church every Sunday but I always go on holidays like Easter and Christmas. My mother is much more devout, particularly since my father died."

"Well, we have something in common — we're both without fathers."

The light changed and they crossed the street. They parted company on the other side. He headed south towards Steeles Avenue and she continued on to the Esplanade, a block away.

Wow, he thought. She's dynamite. She sure stirs me up. Got to watch this. Definitely a no go zone for a rabbi.

He spent the rest of the day poring over Talmudic tracts, losing himself in the views of medieval commentators. He was developing ideas for his first sermons whenever that would be. One he titled provisionally *The Efficacy of Prayer*, a subject stimulated by Alex's joke. Another was *Preservation of our Jewish Heritage*, an outcome of his meeting Rebecca.

Marsha returned at six to prepare supper. "Laura says you bought out the entire Solly's. All I needed was milk, butter and a chala."

"Couldn't help it, Ma. I lost control as soon as I saw the gefilte fish, smoked meat, verenikes, knishes and whatever else I bought."

Marsha kissed him. "You're still my little boy. Tomorrow night is your first Friday back home and when you return from shul, you'll have a traditional Friday night Shabbat dinner."

The evening did not fulfill Ephraim's expectations. It wasn't the food. Marsha lived up to her reputation as the Zimmerman family's best cook. Her chicken soup and matzo balls were delicious, the pickled brisket covered with a thin tomatoey sauce melted in the mouth, the chicken livers chopped with rendered chicken fat and fried onions vanished in seconds, and the roast chicken garnished with whole onions and carrots was superbly moist and tasty and accompanied by a crisp noodle cake and potato knishes.

Walking home after the Friday night service, he had felt light-hearted as he always did at the start of the Sabbath. He entered the apartment singing the hymn welcoming Shabbat and blessing the house. He had looked forward to a Friday evening alone with his mother but to his disappointment found Uncle Avram, Gertie and her husband Irving there.

They enjoyed a pre-dinner schnapps in the living room.

"Did Rebecca call you?" Gertie asked.

Ephraim nodded. "We're having coffee on Sunday."

Uncle Avram downed his whisky in one swallow. "This time don't mess it up."

"Avram," Marsha snapped, "leave my boy alone. Freml will decide who and when he's going to marry, no one else, and definitely not you."

"Marsha, he needs a rich wife. On a rabbi's salary, he can't look after you as well and you can't go on forever at the store. As the song says 'rich or rich, it doesn't matter which girl.'"

Irving filled his glass again and smiled at his father-in-law. "Papa, then I shouldn't have married Gertie. She couldn't put two nickels together."

Avram shook his head vigorously. "It don't apply to you. You're a stockbroker, not a rabbi."

Irving lifted his glass in Ephraim's direction. "Freml, do what I do when he's around. Drink."

Ephraim took a neutral role. "Uncle Avram, I know you're trying to be helpful but I'm not interested in marrying right now. How often do I have to repeat it? I agreed to meet with Rebecca because she seemed anxious to continue our discussion. That's all there is to it."

Avram was not to be put off. "I don't agree. This is a real opportunity. Am I suggesting an ugly girl? No! She is beautiful. Am I suggesting a stupid girl? No! She is very clever and learned. The two of you together will bring simcha to yourselves and your families."

"Oh, Papa, that's enough now," Gertie said. "If it's destined, it will happen and if not, it wasn't destined."

Marsha called them to the dinner table. Ephraim sang the Kiddush — the full grace before the Sabbath meal — then cut the chala and gave everyone a piece. His clear solid baritone voice calmed them down and the meal did the rest. Uncle Avram cheered up and harped no more on the attributes of Rebecca.

Irving regaled them with stories of his many clients. He was of medium height but short by Zimmerman standards. Balding at the temples, he had recently turned forty. Gertie insisted he was as handsome as ever. He was somewhat pot-bellied — a problem, he would explain, caused by too many expense-paid luncheons. Gertie and Irving had met at a friend's wedding a few years ago and had married within months when Gertie became pregnant. They'd left their little boy home with the nanny.

"At the start of somebody's career, Papa, you can't tell about salary," Irving said. "For example, my long time client Mr. Gersovitch tells about how he advised his son when he left high school to become a broker. A few days later the son reports that he has a job in a broker's office. Gersovitch just about has a stroke when it turns out it's a customs broker, not a stock broker. He complains to everyone who will listen how stupid his son is. His son now has a business that's one of the top customs brokers and transport companies in the world. He's a multi-millionaire several times over."

"It's a wonderful story, dear," Gertie said. "But Freml's a rabbi, not a businessman. There's no way he can turn that into a multi-million dollar business."

Irving reached over and patted his wife's head affectionately. "The evangelists have managed to do it."

Laughing, they moved back into the living room. Marsha served tea with lemon and honey cakes. The conversation languished into family gossip. Ephraim listened politely but soon began wishing they would go. Finally, Gertie announced it was time to take her father home.

"You weren't happy tonight," Marsha said as she closed and secured the apartment door. "Was it my cooking?"

Ephraim hugged her. "Your cooking was wonderful. I'm just tired of Uncle Avram and his one track mind. Perhaps I saw too many relatives this week. They are all settled people. Even my younger cousins have chosen careers and are pursuing them without second thoughts. Gertie is happy as a housewife and enjoys teaching piano on the side. I'm still trying to sort out what I should do as a rabbi. There are times when I wonder why I became a rabbi. You've always been a sympathetic sounding board — I was hoping to discuss this with you tonight."

They sat down together on the living room sofa. "Freml, I'm awfully sorry. I didn't realize you were having a problem. Can we talk now?"

"Ma, it's very late. Tomorrow night we're invited to Uncle Syd's. Let's be alone Sunday night."

He confessed to a certain excitement as he headed out on Sunday afternoon to meet Rebecca. There was no doubt he found her attractive, even provocative.

Here I am, he thought, a rabbi, I'm supposed to think about spiritual things, and all I want to do is run my fingers around her bum.

He spotted her before she saw him, sitting at a table in the Food Court near the Tim Horton's counter. Her blonde hair streamed loosely below her shoulders. A pink tank top revealed a seductive expanse of bosom. Her pink skirt fitted tightly around her buttocks and flared out at the thighs. She was in high heels.

She stood up as he approached and made no attempt to hide her admiration. "You look much younger when you're not wearing that pin-stripe suit and that awful hat."

He had put on his beige trousers, open neck shirt, and a tan sports jacket. A red and blue woollen skull cap partly covered his head, fixed in place with a bobby pin. "Flattery will get you anywhere," he said, shaking her hand and kissing her on both cheeks.

They sat down. "A truly orthodox rabbi would not have touched me," she said, frowning.

He nodded. "I have trouble with some of the rules that seem outmoded and not in keeping with today's standards. Not touching a woman because she might be unclean strikes me as treating women as inferior."

Rebecca leaned forward and thumped the table with a fist. "But that's exactly secular thinking,"

Laughing, he held up a hand in a 'stop' gesture. "Hold on. First let me get us some coffee."

They drank their coffee for a few moments in silence. "You accuse me of secular thinking," he said. "I believe men and women are born equal. Some of our rules and traditions imply that women are inferior to men. These I have difficulty with."

"But you can't pick and choose what you'll follow and what you won't. You can't interpret the Torah to suit your own whims."

He shrugged his shoulders. "Why not? We do it all the time. You do it as well. For instance, the Torah is very clear on adultery. The guilty — both men and women — must be stoned to death. Well, how many stonings have we had in Canada recently? Or in Israel? I haven't heard of Jewish lobby groups putting pressure on the government to reintroduce stoning. And when we hear of it happening in other countries, we quite rightly condemn it as barbaric and a throwback to an earlier time."

"Alright," she agreed. "That's an example. I suppose you'll also point out that in Western democracies, we don't put homosexuals to death either even though here too the Torah is quite explicit. In these examples, the law doesn't allow us to carry out the Torah's provisions and we abide by the law."

"Otherwise, you'd want the punishments to proceed?"

She was silent, thoughtfully gazing into her coffee cup as though the answer lay there. "No, I would not agree to such punishments. I don't believe there should be a death penalty for anything. But if you take the approach of examining every line in the Torah to see whether it fits with modern society, you will end up by discarding our entire heritage. The kosher and dietary rules are good examples. They certainly don't fit in to modern society."

"They can be an inconvenience but they don't go against society. On the contrary, if you consider all the diet programs created by weight loss and nutrition experts, our dietary laws are quite simple. I observe them because they're part of us. They set us apart which was presumably God's intention."

She shook her head, frowning. "There you go again. Justifying God's commandments is secular thinking. A truly orthodox Jew accepts the Torah as God's will and doesn't need reasons. What else have you reinterpreted? How about Genesis? Do you accept that the Creation is literally true?"

He leaned forward. "I believe the biblical account is metaphorical and the world is much older than 5,768 years. I believe …"

"But that's the problem," she said, interrupting him. "If you can revise and interpret the Bible as you see fit, why observe any part of it?"

"I'm not revising the Bible. I accept that God created the universe. The Genesis story is how He communicated it to mankind. How could He explain the Big Bang and evolution to ancient people? No, He had to pick a story that would be acceptable at the time, knowing full well that humanity would eventually discover the real mechanism."

She slammed her coffee down, drops splashing onto the table. "There you go — explaining God again. If God had felt early man would not understand, He could have remained silent. Instead the Creation is described in great detail, what He did each day for six days. I suppose in your view, all the miracles are metaphorical — Noah's ark, the splitting of the Red Sea, manna in the desert, the stopping of the sun. Everything can be analyzed and interpreted to suit us — is that what they taught you at Yeshiva U?"

Her tone was scathing and her disgust palpable as she turned sideways in her chair and crossed her legs. Ephraim wondered what Uncle Avram would say if he were present and his lips twitched into a smile.

"It's not funny," she snapped, swinging around to face him. "I can't believe a rabbi would talk the way you do. You said you would perform the marriage ceremony between a Jew and a non-Jew if you felt it was the right thing to do. What about yourself? Would you ever intermarry?"

"Of course not!" He was quite emphatic in his assertion, but as he said it, an image of Laura Burton popped into his mind. A jolt like lightning flowed through him. Gasping in confusion, he leaned over the table and put a hand to his forehead.

Rebecca jumped up and came around the table. "What's wrong? What is it?"

He waved her away. "It's ok. I felt light-headed for a moment. I think I'm drinking too much coffee."

He breathed hard a couple of times, wiped his sweaty forehead with a napkin, and put the image of Laura out of his mind.

"Rebecca, we seem to argue every time we meet. I know these issues are important but I want to discuss them, not argue them. Besides, whether the Creator communicates literally or metaphorically is finally not important. We both believe that however the universe was created, it was God who created it. What we really cherish in the Torah is the moral code that has guided us for thousands of years through all the ups and downs of Jewish history. We shouldn't get sidetracked by debate over the details."

She had remained standing and now walked back to her chair. She looked at him mournfully. "The details are very important to me — they're an essential part of our heritage — they make our heritage. When I teach the children why we celebrate Passover, I tell them all about Moses and how he led us out of slavery. I do not teach them that according to some historians, no record of Moses outside the Bible has ever been found and therefore he may not have existed, that the story of Moses may be metaphorical as you might argue. That would reduce our Bible heritage to the same level as Greek mythology."

Ephraim nodded. "I see your point. Let's get off the Bible. Tell me about your school plans."

He couldn't help but admire her as she animatedly described the school she would hopefully open one day. It would be a girls' school starting at

Kindergarten and going right through High School. The curriculum would include both Jewish and secular subjects.

"Unlike the typical parochial school which segregates the religious and secular side, say, into morning and afternoon classes, my timetable will integrate the two so that students will understand that the two are all part of living. I plan to emphasize Hebrew but not only on the Jewish side. Some of the secular subjects will be taught in Hebrew to demonstrate that it can be used in everyday life, not only in Israel."

"Cool. You're really ambitious. You'll have to import teachers from Israel."

She nodded and looked hard at him. "Some. But there are people here who could teach in Hebrew."

He smiled. "If that's a job offer, I'll definitely consider it. I presume it'll be a few years before you can launch your school."

"Yes, I want to get more teaching experience first. Then I have to find sponsors and raise enough funds for bricks and mortar and to hire expensive people like you."

They left the Food Court and walked slowly, chatting amiably, towards the exit where Rebecca had parked. Obligingly, he installed her number in his cell phone.

He held the car door open for her. As she seated herself, her skirt rose up and revealed a well-formed shapely knee and thigh. She looked up at him, smiling coquettishly. "Would you like a lift home?"

"No, thanks," he said and saw disappointment written on her face. "My mother will be upset if I don't visit her in the store."

The store was crowded. He saw his mother working with some customers, a saleswoman he didn't know was behind the cash ringing in sales, and then Laura walked around a display case with a male shopper in tow. Once again he felt a flush of excitement race through him. He stood there trying to control his emotions, struggling to blot out the desire to grasp her, hold her, kiss her. He focused on the rallying call of Judaism — "Hear O Israel, the Lord is our God, the Lord is One." He watched the Hebrew words form in front of him, over and over, until he could walk calmly into the store.

Laura saw him, and without interrupting her conversation with the customer, waved at him. The quick smile and the sparkle in her eyes almost cost him his control. He turned resolutely to seek out his mother, but she was still very busy.

Laura had succeeded with her customer and was leading him to the cash desk, carrying an armful of cream coloured dishes. While the customer paid, Laura gift-wrapped the purchase. Ephraim admired how quickly the wrapping paper enclosed the dishes, ribbons attached, and the whole carefully placed in a large paper shopper.

His mother called him over. "Ephraim, honey, Mrs Gillicuddy has bought a set of the Provence dishes and two of the large wall clocks and needs help to get them to her car. Mrs. Gillicuddy, this is my son."

Somewhat plump and not very tall, Mrs Gillicuddy was a youngish woman with a small child. "Nice to meet you. My husband was called into work today so I have to do all the shopping. There's one clock for my mother, one for my mother-in-law and the dishes my darling little boy is buying for me."

"Mrs. Gillicuddy," Marsha said, laughing, "your little boy shows remarkably good taste."

Marsha, Laura and the other saleswoman carefully gift wrapped the purchases. When the parcels were ready, Ephraim carried the dishes in two large bags, while Mrs. Gillicuddy and Laura each carried a clock.

"I know you'll be careful with the dishes," Mrs. Gillicuddy said as they walked through the mall.

"Don't worry, Mrs. Gillicuddy," Laura said. "They're in safe hands. Mr Zimmerman is a rabbi."

Mrs. Gillicuddy stopped and looked at him. "Are you really? I've never been helped by a rabbi before. I must tell my parish priest and see what he's going to do for me."

Laura smiled gaily up at him. "There you have it, Mr. Zimmerman. You've started a competition between the clergy. Who knows where this will end."

As they walked back to the store, Ephraim said to Laura, "Please call me by my first name. Calling me by my last name or rabbi makes me feel terribly old."

"It's funny," she said. "My image of rabbis was always of old, white bearded men. I never thought they could be so young and sexy…" She stopped, embarrassed, blushing. "I'm sorry. I'm speaking out of turn again. My mother says it's my only fault."

They were standing on the escalator descending to the lower level where the store was located. Ephraim smiled at her. "My mother says I don't speak my mind enough — that I'm too quiet."

"On average then, we're just about right."

Their laughter caught the attention of a tall man, standing in front of the store, staring into the display window. He turned and looked suspiciously at them, then leaned over and kissed Laura briefly on the lips.

"Ephraim, this is my boyfriend, Frank Yanovich."

Ephraim reached out a hand, but Frank ignored it. In a gravelly, accented voice, he demanded of Laura. "Where ya bin? I don't see you in store. You ready soon?"

Frank was quite tall, with a bluff, blond square face, lips pressed grimly together. A dark double breasted suit emphasized his broad shoulders and muscular torso. A silk blue-striped tie hung from the collar of his starched white shirt.

"Ephraim is my employer's son," Laura admonished Frank. "He's also a rabbi. I think a little courtesy is required."

Frank responded by nodding to Ephraim.

"The store closes in fifteen minutes, Frank. If we're not busy, Mrs. Zimmerman will let me off a little early." Turning to Ephraim, she explained, "Frank is taking me and my mother to a poshy restaurant for Sunday night dinner."

"Very nice," Ephraim said, smiling at Frank. "Have a pleasant evening."

Ephraim and Laura entered the store while Frank waited outside. There were still a few customers taking advantage of the closing minutes.

"Ephraim, do you still remember how to work the cash register?" his mother asked. He nodded and went behind the cash desk. "Then Laura can go."

He drove home with his mother.

"How did your meeting go?" Marsha asked.

"Meeting? It wasn't a meeting. I simply walked with her to Mrs. Gillicuddy's car and back."

Marsha twisted in her seat, nearly careening the Cadillac off the road. "Freml, what are you talking about?"

Ephraim exploded in a nervous giggle. He'd been so enthralled by his brush with Laura, he'd forgotten all about Rebecca. "Ah, yes, Rebecca. We argued vehemently for the first half-hour. Uncle Avram would've had a breakdown. Then we talked very nicely the rest of the time. Ma, I could see marrying her if I wanted to marry now. Her school idea is ambitious and like her, aggressive. There's even a job for me. I have her phone number and I'll definitely call her one of these days. Use a diplomatic expression when you're telling Uncle Avram — 'there was a forthright exchange of views and scope for continuing contact.'"

Marsha laughed. "And I know what Avram will say — 'the boy is mishuga.'"

While Marsha prepared dinner, he said the afternoon prayers alone in his bedroom. He had difficulty concentrating and mumbled the words without focussing on their meaning. Images of the two women kept flashing through his mind — both enticing, but one more alluring than the other. He kept returning to the moment when he insisted to Rebecca he would never intermarry. The thought of Laura Burton had stopped him cold. Could it be that all his learning, all his convictions, all his principles were corruptible in an instant by lust?

The ringing of his cell phone brought him back to his prayers but he couldn't answer it at that moment. He heard the phone ring in another part of the house.

Dinner was on the table when he finished. He made the blessing over the bread and they began to eat. It was his favourite Sunday night dinner — salmon cakes and potato latkes.

"That was Rebecca on the phone, worried about you. What happened today? She said you nearly fainted. I'm to cut back your coffee consumption."

He speared a latke onto his plate. "It was just a momentary weakness. Nothing to be alarmed about. It's got nothing to do with coffee — that's what I told her. We had launched into a conversation about our beliefs. I was suddenly overwhelmed by all my doubts and the realization absolutely shocked me."

Marsha stopped eating and laid down her fork and knife. "Sweetheart, what do you doubt?"

"At times, everything. When I'm praying or reading the Torah or studying the Talmud, I'm ok. It all makes sense and I understand what it means to be Jewish and why I became a rabbi. Then I feel like an Israelite of old, trudging happily through the desert, fed by heaven, and led by a leader whose every utterance is holy. When I'm away from the books and start thinking about it, I wonder whether it's all true and which side of the line Moses drew in the sand I would stand on."

He cut away at a salmon cake and stuffed it into his mouth. He smiled at his mother who was looking at him, her brow furrowed in lines of worry. "The one thing I never lose faith in is your cooking. This is excellent."

"Do you even doubt the existence of God?" Marsha asked.

"Sometimes. At least, I wonder about it. You look around the world and there's so much evil. If a God exists, would He allow such terrible things? You know, that's what Kabbalah is all about — why is God's creation imperfect? But then I think — who am I to tell God how to run His universe? And yet, I'd like to see some evidence that there is indeed a Supreme Intelligence directing things. Alex doesn't think so. He says God did the Big Bang and not only provided all the matter but all the physical laws and what we have is what's evolved and we have to make the best of it.

"In my last year at Yeshiva U, I met a very old man, well in his eighty's. He was kind of a professor emeritus and gave a seminar on the Kabbalah. On a very warm day in March, he removed his jacket and rolled up his sleeves. I saw the number tattooed on his arm. After the class was over, I talked to him about his Holocaust experience. He was imprisoned in 1941 and survived because he was put to work as a slave labourer. There were 6,059 young men and boys in his work detail. On the last High Holidays before Auschwitz was liberated, they killed 2,000 each day of Rosh Hashanah and on Yom Kippur. There were only fifty-nine left in his group to greet the liberators. 'It was then that I lost my faith that a God existed,' he said. I asked him, 'But if you've lost your faith, why have you taught all these years at the Yeshiva and you still observe the religion?' 'Because I'm Jewish,' he answered. 'They took away my God but they will never take away my race.' Ma, I don't want to be like that. If I doubt the existence of a Supreme Being, then there's nothing to pray to or for and all our holy books have historical and literary merit but no religious significance."

Marsha shook her head. "Sweetheart, you cannot reach such a conclusion just because there's evil in the world. Even in your Kabbalah rabbi's case, he was spared. Was the hand of God not behind his rescue?"

"I'd like to believe that, Ma." Ephraim forked the last piece of latke and chewed away thoughtfully. "Or was it just plain luck?"

Marsha reached out and stroked his cheek. "My sweet little boy, I'm sorry to see you in such turmoil. If it makes you feel better, I have no such doubts. The fact that we have survived centuries of persecution, and the Holocaust and are thriving and have our own country is all the proof I need that a God exists and watches over us. Have you ever discussed this with your teachers?"

"Yes — there was one rabbi with whom I felt I could talk. Big mistake. He concluded I was a mental case and lined me up with a therapist. I went to one session with the therapist who felt I had a mild case of bi-polar. When I was up, I was a believer — when I was down, I had doubts. I tried to explain that it was doubt that drove me down, not down that drove me to doubt. To no avail — the diagnosis stood. Fortunately, I was at the end of my studies there so I was given a letter to consult a psychologist when I returned to Canada. You're my shrink, Ma."

Marsha's brow furrowed even deeper. "Freml, it's not a joking matter. Perhaps you should see someone."

Ephraim carried the now empty dishes away to the kitchen sink and poured the coffee.

He had anticipated his mother's reaction. He, too, had worried about the therapist's diagnosis and had spent several sleepless nights engrossed in its denial. He had debated whether to disclose it to his mother. Why worry her? Since the diagnosis gnawed at him — of course, it would bother his mother. But it was all nonsense and, for his own mental stability, had to be dismissed.

"Ma, there's nothing wrong with me. Everybody has ups and downs. Even you look depressed when you've had a lousy sales day. Or when you're buying a product and you're not sure it will sell. Well, I'm in business too. My product is inspiration and religious conviction — that's what I sell. If I lose confidence in my product then — yes — I get depressed, confused, unhappy. Getting on top of the doubt will cure the disease. It's that simple."

They drank their coffee in silence. Marsha drained her cup and placed it carefully back on the saucer. "I don't know how to help you. All I can offer is a mother's love and concern. I do so want to see you happy and settled. It's what your father would want too. If your doubts persist and you feel you cannot continue as a rabbi, then so be it. I am always on your side, no matter what."

Ephraim hugged and kissed her. "You've already helped, Ma. Just being able to talk about my belief issues with you leaves me somehow at peace. Now, you go relax in the living room and I'll finish cleaning up."

EPHRAIM

Lying in bed, Ephraim shifted uneasily under the hard, thoughtful stare of Elijah. The prophet shook his head and reached up with long, bony fingers to stroke his beard.

"So, you believe your problem is that you have encountered two women, both fair in face and form and, in your view, both promise carnal delight. This is not your problem. As Abraham and others did, wed them both."

"But Prophet Elijah, I can wed only one and the one I truly like is not of our religion. That is what troubles me."

Elijah shook his head emphatically. "My son, wed the Israelite and keep the other as a concubine. That is what Jacob did. Leah and Rachel were his lawful spouses and their handmaidens also graced his bed and delivered him children. Remember, the Almighty has promised that we, the Chosen People, will become as numerous as the grains of sand bordering the sea or as the stars in the sky. It is the children who will fulfill this promise. Your children — no matter who bears them — must follow the path laid out by the One and observe His commandments.

"However, that is not the problem that concerns me. It is your equivocation in matters of belief that disturbs me." Elijah stood up and leaning over the bed, touched Ephraim's head. "Get your house in order. I must go now."

Ephraim threw off the covers and swinging his feet out, sat up and reached out a restraining arm. "Wait. I need to talk it through." He clutched at Elijah's robe and felt the fabric disintegrate.

Elijah looked at him sadly. "There is nothing to talk through."

The golden haze evaporated. For long moments, Ephraim sat on the edge of his bed, sweat pimpling his forehead, dripping into his eyes. Then he fell back, fast asleep, his feet still touching the floor.

CHAPTER 3

Rabbis Without Borders

If a bearded man can be described as cherubic, then Rabbi Sholom Nitsky fitted the description. He was short and pudgy, and angelic innocence flooded out of the brown eyes framed by twinkle lines. Ephraim felt the warmth of his benign smile and friendly greeting and took an instant liking to him.

The world headquarters of the Chevra Kadisha Institute was located on Bathurst Street near Lawrence Avenue in a second storey flat over a kosher butcher shop.

"Excuse the modesty of our Head Office," Rabbi Nitsky said. "Our donors don't like us working in a lavish setting. They want more of their money to go to people like you — the front line workers."

Ephraim laughed. "What can I say?"

Nitsky's office was the windowless back half of a double living room, partitioned from the front half. It was lit by neon lights. Nitsky sat behind a worn steel desk, covered in files and paper. He motioned to Ephraim to pull a chair from a small conference table, the only other furniture in the room.

"Before we go any further, let me introduce you to my helpers." He stood up, walked around the desk, and opened a door in the partition. Ephraim could see several desks in the light that came through the window fronting Bathurst Street. "Ladies, come meet our new recruit."

Ephraim stood up as three women came through the door. The first was a tiny woman with greying hair and a large welcoming smile.

"This is Dora, my wife. She is the head administrator. If ever you have problems in the field other than religious problems, she is the one you contact."

"Even if you have religious problems," said Dora, "call me first. I always remind him where to look up the answers."

Nitsky laughed. "Now, now, Dora. This lady is Mrs. Gottlieb, she assists Dora."

Mrs. Gottlieb was a much older woman. She merely nodded.

"And last but not least, we have Miss Smith. She is our bookkeeper and comes in once a week to straighten us out. Even though Miss Smith is not Jewish, she assures me her accounts are kosher."

Miss Smith, a thin youngish woman, gave a resigned smile — Ephraim guessed this was not the first time she'd heard the remark.

"Ladies, it's a pleasure to meet you," Ephraim said. "I'm sure I'll need your help. I'm not only new to this organization, but I've only just become a rabbi."

"We know something about you, Rabbi Zimmerman," Dora said. "My father teaches Kabbalah at Yeshiva University and he spoke very highly about you. He thinks you're the most brilliant graduate they've had in a while." Rabbi Nitsky smiled and nodded.

"Your father is Toiviah Gruenberg?" Ephraim marvelled at the coincidence.

"Yes. He also appreciated how interested you were in his Holocaust experiences. He says we're very lucky to get you." Nitsky smiled and nodded again.

"Well, I hope I can live up to everyone's expectations. But, I have to confess, I was disturbed by your father's loss of faith that a God exists."

Dora shook her head and laughed. "Don't believe it. He's angry with God, but he still believes no matter what he says. Isn't that right, Sholom?"

"My wife is right. I've had many talks with him over the years. He is angry as a son is sometimes angry with a father when he believes the father has been unfair. But just as the son doesn't question the existence of the father, neither does my father-in-law in his heart of hearts. Anyway, it's time these ladies get back to work and we still have a lot to discuss."

"It's a lot more complicated than I thought," Ephraim told Marsha, as they ate supper. "Nitsky emphasized that it was difficult to find kosher food in the hinterland and that I might find myself subsisting on tomato and lettuce sandwiches. The Institute actually sends out food to the rabbis in the field but it may not always arrive on time. Nitsky says that people will invite me to eat at their house but their food may not be scrupulously kosher. He wants me to go easy on my parishioners. They probably don't observe all the rules and if I get too fussy, I may find myself shut out.

"Then he told me a joke. A congregation is looking to hire a rabbi. They ask the first candidate, 'You come to the synagogue on the Sabbath and lying on the steps is a $50 dollar bill. What would you do?' 'I would leave it there. You can't touch money on the Sabbath.' The congregation rejects the candidate as not being practical enough. The second candidate replies, 'I would pick it up. God obviously left it there.' They reject him — he's not religious enough. They hire the third candidate who says, 'I'll let you know when the time comes.' Nitsky wants me to remember this story."

Marsha laughed, spluttering and coughing as she was in the midst of swallowing. "Your Rabbi Nitsky sounds like a very wise man. Would you like to invite him and his wife for a meal?"

"Sure, you'll enjoy them. This weekend, he wants me to go with him to Guernsey. It's a small town on Lake Huron, about a three-hour drive. He says I'll get some first hand field experience. They have a synagogue but no permanent rabbi. We'll leave Friday morning after the morning prayers and be back Sunday afternoon."

Marsha frowned in disappointment. "You promised me you'd be around all summer."

Ephraim walked around the table and put an arm around her shoulder. "Ma, it's only for a couple of days, although I may go with him to other towns during the summer. Ma, I've got to start practising my profession."

"I know, sweetheart. I'm so busy at the store that I hardly have time to be with you. At least, it's not for a few days yet that you'll be away."

He returned to his seat and poured the coffee. "We're going in Sholom Nitsky's car and his wife is joining us. We're also participating in the Sunday Morning Breakfast Club at the synagogue which is why I won't be home until the afternoon."

Marsha sighed. "When Laura gets more experience, I'll come with you on a trip. I would love to see you in action. I would be your best listener when you make your sermon."

Ephraim grinned. "Probably the only listener."

Over the next two days, he prepared himself for the weekend. From his laptop, he accessed a web site through a password Sholom had given him. He studied the bios of the key people he would meet in Guernsey. He wrote out a first draft of his sermon and took it to the store, hoping he could drag his mother away for fifteen minutes to get her input.

"Mrs. Zimmerman's gone home," Laura explained. "You must have just missed her. She felt tired."

Ephraim stood there, nonplussed, not knowing what to say, trying to suppress the flow of desire that raced through him. She smiled at him, her eyes shining and beguiling.

"You look so disappointed," she said as he remained silent. "I hope it wasn't something serious."

Nothing serious, he thought, just four years of intense study in danger of crumbling.

"No," he managed to get out. "I wanted to review my sermon with her. It will be my first one this Saturday. I'm a little nervous about it."

"I'd love to read it," Laura said. "Would I understand it or is it in Jewish?"

"It's mostly in English, but there are occasional Jewish and Hebrew words." He found himself wanting to prolong the contact and hesitantly held out the sermon. She took it from him.

"Am I being too forward?" she asked, noticing his reluctance. "I've actually done this before. I came first in my public speaking class at the retail course. We had to research a product from a grocery shelf and then talk for fifteen minutes, trying to convince fellow students to buy the product."

She perched on the stool behind the counter and began to read. He watched her as she read it, concentrating and totally absorbed. He wanted desperately to put his arms around her and clasp her to him. Now and then she asked him to explain an expression.

"In the joke, you refer to a lemele. What's that?"

"It's a guy who's kind of awkward, bumbling, shy, socially inept, women don't flock to him."

She smiled at him. "Not like you, I bet."

"I understand what you're getting at," she said after finishing. "Your message is — if you pray to God, make sure it's for something important like world peace or for the recovery of the sick and dying. The joke you start off is very funny. Your sermon would be just as meaningful to a Christian audience. I give you an A+."

Ephraim laughed delightedly as he took back the sermon and reached out to shake her hand. "Thank you for reading it and for the high mark." Her hand in his was slim and dainty. He held it longer than he should and she made no effort to withdraw it. A customer entered the store. Ephraim mumbled "Thank you" and "Goodbye" as he left.

What am I doing?he thought as he walked quickly home. She likes me, too. But it can't go further. It's got to stop. I must stay away from the store. He arrived home, sweaty from the exertion, with a sense of deep despair.

Marsha was in the living room reading the newspaper. He poured himself a whiskey and joined her while she went over the sermon.

"It's excellent," she said. "You can trust a mother's unbiased view. But you seem a little upset. Don't worry. Everyone will like you and your sermon. Relax while I make supper."

His cell phone rang. "Are you ok?I haven't heard from you." Rebecca did not waste time with opening hellos.

He told her about his meeting with Nitsky and his upcoming debut in Guernsey. "I'd love to read your sermon. May I come over after supper?"

When she arrived he was in the midst of the evening prayers in the solitude of his bedroom and she sat in the living room talking to Marsha.

When he joined them, he reached out to grasp Rebecca's hand which she quickly withdrew.

"It's not right for you to touch me. You still haven't learned."

Marsha looked at her enquiringly. "Rebecca, it's only the very orthodox who have such strict rules."

Rebecca shook her head emphatically. "Mrs. Zimmerman, any departure from our traditions is secular thinking and must be confronted and corrected."

"Oh, come on, Rebecca," Ephraim snapped. "Lighten up. I'm really not in the mood for another lengthy debate.I'm going to run my religion as I see fit and in a way that makes sense for me. I don't mind discussing your views and if any register with me, I'm adjustable. If this is too difficult for you to accept —." he paused.

Rebecca's eyes filled with tears and he immediately regretted the harshness of his tone.

"Freml, that's no way to talk to a lady who wants to help you. Now let Rebecca read the sermon. First, would you like a cup of tea?"

Rebecca nodded and Ephraim was dispatched to the kitchen.

"I think your sermon is wonderful," she said when he returned and poured the tea. "Especially I like the part where you tell business people not to pray for financial success — 'if you're smart enough to get into business, you should be smart enough to pull it off.' The Almighty is there to help you when you most need it. If you were in my first grade class, I'd give you five stars."

Ephraim smiled his appreciation. "Thanks. I'm glad you like it. I don't know why I'm so nervous about this weekend. I guess it's my debut, even though it's a small synagogue in an out-of-the-way town. I'm confident in my ability to lead the service and to read the Torah. But the sermon was something else — it had to be memorable, not just a bunch of trite clichés."

Rebecca squeezed lemon into her tea. "You're too hard on yourself. Your writing is excellent. Despite our disagreements, I can tell your command of our religion is strong. Gertie tells me you graduated first in your class so I know you're very clever. Therefore, I will not accept false modesty from you."

Marsha clapped her hands. "There you are, Freml, and she's a teacher."

Ephraim bowed low. "I accept your remarks with humility — even if my humility is false."

Giggling, Rebecca wagged a finger at him.

"Tell me about your school plans," Marsha suggested.

They spent the rest of the evening listening to Rebecca's ideas for the school and its curriculum. When she got up to go, Ephraim accompanied her to her car.

"I'm sorry I spoke to you the way I did," he said as the elevator door closed behind them. "I'm feeling very unsettled at the moment and I'm afraid I took my anxiety out on the nearest target."

"That's ok," she replied. "I'm uneasy at times about my plans for the school and whether I can really pull it off. I react by getting stubborn."

He held the car door open as she took her seat. She looked up to him and he leaned over and kissed her on the lips. "I'll call you Sunday night and tell you how I made out." He waved as she drove off. *This time she didn't object to my touching her,* he thought.

"I don't know what your intentions are," Marsha admonished him when he returned to the apartment, "but you have to be nice to her. Take my word for it. She's in love with you. She never took her eyes off you. If you don't think she's for you, let her down gently."

Ephraim nodded. "Ma, I don't know how I feel about her. She's attractive in every respect — beautiful, spirited, smart, educated. And I do like her. Until I sort myself out, I don't want to get involved. That's why this weekend is so important to me. It's my first real test."

At nine o'clock on Friday morning, Ephraim, suitcase in hand, waited at the kerb outside the apartment building. A minivan pulled towards him and, perhaps because of the play of light on its windshield, seemed to have neither driver nor passenger. Then Ephraim saw Sholom's small head peering over the steering wheel. Dora was a diminutive shadow nestled beside him. Ephraim suppressed a smile as he got into the car and settled in the seat behind Sholom.

They chatted cheerfully as the car sped west on Steeles Avenue and turned down Dufferin to the 401, the highway that slices through the populated part of Ontario from the Quebec to the US border. Until they cleared Toronto, the traffic was intense and they moved along bumper-to-bumper. Once west of the city, they drove swiftly towards their destination.

The synagogue was on a busy street in the downtown district of Guernsey. Ephraim was surprised by the size of the building — it seemed large for the relatively small Jewish population of the town and the villages around it. A Star of David graced the window over the entrance door and higher up, painted on the wall, was the double tablet symbolic expression of the Ten Commandments. The synagogue was locked. They waited in the minivan until a car drove in and stopped beside them in the small parking lot adjoining the synagogue.

"Sorry you had to wait. Sholom, you drove too fast. I wasn't expecting you so soon."

Sholom laughed. "Ephraim, meet Joe Petrov, the President of the shul. Joe believes the best defence is offence. We've had many arguments over whether sin is the fault of Man or a problem caused by the Almighty for setting the bar too high."

"I always lose the argument," Joe said as he shook Ephraim's hand and kissed Dora on the forehead. A thoroughly good-natured man was Ephraim's quick assessment. Joe was an imposing figure, as tall as Ephraim, round featured, and dressed in full suit and tie. He was hatless but put on a skull cap as he showed them into the synagogue.

"Our shul is larger than we need today." They stood in the centre aisle between two rows of pews, facing the raised area and the reader's desk. Behind the desk was the curtained enclosure containing the Torah scrolls. Chandeliers hung from the high ceiling. "The congregation is aging as our young people move out, mostly to Toronto. Also, we can't afford a cantor, so you have to lead the service and sing the best you can. As far as our religious habits are concerned, I'm sure Sholom has explained to you that men and women sit together in our service. Also, all our members live further north along the lake, so they'll come by car. For you, I've arranged rooms at the downtown motel which is a ten minute walk from here. Of course, for your meals, you're invited to join me and my wife — we keep a kosher home."

Sholom nodded. "As always, that's very kind of you, Joe. I'd like Ephraim to lead the services tonight and tomorrow and to give the sermon, if that's ok with you. Your shul is his debut stage."

"At least we'll be able to see him when he gets behind the podium," Joe said, chuckling

Hilda Petrov welcomed them warmly as they arrived for lunch. As tall as her husband, middle-aged plump, she had to lean over to embrace Dora. She examined Ephraim. "So you're the new rabbi. All the young ones will swoon when they see you. Maybe even the older ones."

Their home was at the end of a leafy driveway off the shore road that extended north from Guernsey. It overlooked the beach and the narrowing lake as it funnelled towards the St. Clair River. Hilda served them on the patio. Far out on the water, the occasional lake ship went by. Seagulls swirled and whirled in the cloudless blue sky, then skimmed low over the surface hunting for prey. It was still too cold to swim, but hikers strolled along the beach. Here and there a white sail speckled the blue water.

"What an idyllic setting," Ephraim said. "The Almighty has certainly blessed you."

"Yes, we love it here," Joe agreed. "The Almighty did the backdrop, but Hilda and I take credit for the house."

Sholom wagged a finger at Joe. "There you go again. You never give full credit to the Almighty for your success."

"You're right, Sholom. This time I have to give the Almighty full credit for the way the house turned out. To save money, I hired the worst contractor in the area and somehow he did a great job."

The house was indeed a large, yet cosy looking cottage, set in the midst of spacious gardens. Spring flowers blossomed in the beddings circling the house and the lawn swept green to the low stone wall abutting the sandy beach.

An image flashed into Ephraim's mind. Ensconced in this house and by his side, gracing both their lives, was a woman he loved. He couldn't see Rebecca fitting the bill — her ambition required a much larger playing field. Laura would be ideal and the thought did not need much persuasion.

He pulled his mind back to the conversation.

"Remember, Rabbi Ephraim, go easy on us. We can't all be orthodox in this small town. We're lucky to have a synagogue. Hilda and I keep a kosher home but it means bringing food in from Toronto and the cost is high. Few of the others even bother. Also, a lot of our people here are scientists, engineers, PhDs, and other professionals. They break the rules because they consider themselves freethinkers. Yet they still support the synagogue."

Wow, thought Ephraim, Rebecca would have a field day here fighting secular thinking.

"I see you're smiling," Joe commented. "Please take what I said seriously."

"Not to worry, Joe." Ephraim put a reassuring hand on Joe's shoulder. "I'm quite tolerant and liberal. No, I was thinking about a young woman I met recently who considers any deviation from tradition as aiding and abetting the secular trend. She even gives me a hard time."

"Talking about a young woman," Hilda said, "Joe, tell them about the speaker the sisterhood arranged for Sunday morning."

"I don't know whether to call them the sisterhood or the motherhood," Joe said. "They've invited a girl from Toronto who would like to test an idea she has for a Jewish parochial school. She'll make her presentation at the Sunday Morning Breakfast Club."

A cauldron of ugly anger began to bubble and boil inside Ephraim and threatened to erupt. He stared grimly out at the scenery, his jaw set, his lips pressed together. He didn't doubt Rebecca's real motive. He wasn't flattered — he felt stalked. All his expectations of an exciting and satisfying start to his career were on the verge of collapse. For a split second, he considered excusing himself on some pretext and heading for home. Then he got control of himself and suppressed his anger. He turned to Sholom. "Too bad we didn't know. We could have offered her a lift."

"She's flying down Saturday night after Shabbat," Hilda said. "She's staying at a motel near the airport."

Joe drove them back to their hotel. They had several hours before the Sabbath began. Sholom and Dora went to their room. Ephraim, feeling lethargic after the lunch, opted for a walk along the riverfront. His cell phone rang.

Marsha sounded uneasy. "Freml, I'm calling to tell you that Rebecca is going to Guernsey for the Sunday morning get together. I don't want you to be surprised."

Ephraim sat down on a park bench beside the walkway and squinted up into the westering sun. "It's ok, Ma. I already knew. I'm not happy about it but I won't let it get in my way. I'll find the opportunity for a quiet chat with her."

"Well, don't blame her too much. Avram told me proudly how he thought of the idea and persuaded Rebecca. Gertie knows somebody in Guernsey and talked them into inviting Rebecca. I told both Avram and Gertie it was time they minded their own business."

The Friday night service was poorly attended. By including both men and women, they were able to form a minyin — the required quorum of ten for public prayer. Several more people dropped in after the service began.

Ephraim looked out over the podium at the near empty pews. This is what my itinerant rabbinical life will be like, he thought — preaching to the few in synagogues that once reflected a more prosperous time.

Nevertheless, he held nothing back. His baritone voice echoed around the hall, its sonority grandly welcoming Queen Sabbath. The congregation listened in rapt attention, joining in with gusto during the responsive parts.

Afterwards, several of the latecomers took him aside. "That was great, Rabbi," a young man offered. "When Rabbi Nitsky's in charge, it's a service — with you, it's a concert."

Ephraim, Sholom and Dora followed Hilda and Joe into the basement of the synagogue. "We know you won't drive out to our house on the Sabbath," Hilda said, "so we brought all the food here."

The basement was for entertaining with a large kitchen and a spacious hall. A table was set for seven people just outside the kitchen. The Petrov's two children — a pretty sixteen year old girl and a tall eighteen year old boy — joined them. Sholom recited the Kiddush and blessed the bread. The meal was the traditional Friday night dinner with chicken soup, matzo balls, roast chicken and vegetables and a sweet lokshin kugel, completed with tea and honey cakes.

As always, at the start of the Sabbath, Ephraim was elated, light-hearted and joyful. The Friday night service had gone exceptionally well. In addition, he was amongst friends, basking in the warmth and confidence they radiated towards him and towards each other. Rebecca had diminished to a smudge on the horizon of an otherwise cloudless sky.

Dora, quiet most of the day, now prattled incessantly and busily interrogated the children on their plans for the future. The eighteen-year old was graduating from High School and had been accepted at the University of Western Ontario, a little over an hour's drive away.

"That means," Joe said, "he can come home on weekends, do his laundry and get a square meal."

"These are great people," Ephraim said to Sholom and Dora, as they walked slowly back to their hotel. "I'm happy you brought me here."

Sholom chuckled. "Don't get too comfortable. This is the place where Dora and I give new recruits a final look over before sending them far and wide."

The orthodox Saturday morning service takes about three hours. Wearing long black robes and full skullcaps, the two rabbis followed Joe and the deacon onto the raised area and took their seats on either side of the Torah ark. Sholom insisted on leading the service during the first hour which began at nine am. There were enough worshippers for a quorum and the number kept growing as latecomers arrived. When Ephraim took over, all the front pews halfway to the back were filled. As Hilda had predicted, there were many young female faces looking expectantly up at him.

"Your fame has spread," Joe whispered as Ephraim walked past the President's chair to the podium. "We haven't had a crowd like this since the High Holidays."

Ephraim announced the appropriate page number and the next prayer in the siddur — the traditional prayer book. "Those of you who have difficulty with Hebrew may read the English translation. While God prefers Hebrew, He values participation above all. He won't be confused if the message comes in two languages." Over the ripple of laughter, he sang the opening prayer, the words rolling easily off his tongue and amplified by his strong baritone voice.

EPHRAIM

The service progressed to the moment when the Torah is read. He exulted as the heavy scroll, sheathed in its cloth dress, its top handles crowned in silver, was removed from the shelter of the curtained ark and handed to him. This lengthy parchment document, copied assiduously by hand, generation after generation, was the living connection binding him to the earliest Israelites. As he read the portion of the Torah prescribed for that Sabbath, he revelled in the knowledge that he was reading the writing of ancient scribes, carefully imprinting the oral record of Man's encounters with God.

His state of ecstasy was contagious. The worshippers listened spellbound as he flawlessly sang the portion, following the stylized tones that were also part of the tradition.

His sermon was well received. There was laughter at the jokes and nods of agreement and approval as he made his points.

After the service, he greeted a line up of congregants with a hand shake and the usual "Shabbat shalom!" The women who met him expressed disappointment when he said he was leaving the next day after the Breakfast Club. Alex will die with envy when I tell him, Ephraim thought.

"You were excellent," Sholom said to him as they descended the basement steps for lunch. Dora nodded in emphatic agreement. "We are pleased and proud to have you with us at the Chevra Kadisha Institute."

Sunday morning, the Sabbath over, they drove to the synagogue. Ephraim felt good about himself. His successful Shabbat performance had gone a long way to quieting his doubts and bolstering his confidence. Rebecca's firmness of belief and intransigence, her ambition and aggressiveness, had intimidated him. But now he had demonstrated to his own satisfaction that he could attract and nudge people along to appreciate the important Judaic traditions. The many details of religious observance that Rebecca defended in order to thwart the secular trend were really not that important. So what if men and women sat together during the service. Surely, the aim was to get them to the service. And if they were comfortable in English — would the Almighty really care? He felt vindicated, almost smug.

Yet it rankled him when Rebecca entered the basement hall. The buzz of conversation came to an abrupt halt. She was wearing a light blue dress with a pink scarf at her throat. Her long blonde hair fell glistening half way down her back. She carried a heavy bag draped over one shoulder and pulled a small wheeled suitcase.

"Joe, get your eyes back in your head and greet our guest speaker," Hilda commanded. Dutifully, Joe shook hands with Rebecca and introduced her around.

The sisterhood of the synagogue had set up a table with coffee, honey cakes, Danish pastries and muffins. The Breakfast Clubbers — Ephraim recognized many of them from the day before — were helping themselves. Ephraim was busily chatting with a trio of young women when Joe brought Rebecca over. Ephraim reached out and shook her hand. Rebecca offered no objection but looked at him uneasily.

"We know each other," Ephraim explained to Joe. "Rebecca takes piano lessons from my cousin. We've discussed her school idea and I think you'll find it very interesting."

"Ephraim, can you help me set up?" Rebecca asked, apologizing to the young women for dragging him away.

He followed Joe and Rebecca to the far end of the hall. Rebecca took from the large bag a small overhead projector and power point slides and placed them on a table close to the stage where Joe was setting up a screen. Joe left them to shepherd the audience to their seats.

They got the projector going and Ephraim tested the focus on the screen.

Rebecca looked at him, the uneasy look back on her face. "You're angry with me. I can tell. I don't know why. I have as much right to be here as you do. I need practice in presenting the school so when I go after Toronto donors, I'll be professional and businesslike. Your uncle thought this would be a good place for me to start — especially since you would be here and could help."

He had hoped she would show some contrition, some understanding of his feelings.

"I agree entirely with you," he said. "You can pursue your cause whenever and wherever you want. I will help you in any way I can. All you have to do is ask me — not my uncle or Gertie. I just don't want to feel like I'm the butt of some conspiracy."

Although he had spoken firmly but not harshly, he felt immediate pangs of regret as he saw her lower lip quiver. They were interrupted as the Breakfast Clubbers joined them.

EPHRAIM

Ephraim watched in admiration as Rebecca presented her school idea, explaining confidently and easily its purpose, its structure and mode of operation.

"I see you're all eagerly reaching for your wallets," she concluded. "However, at this point, I'm not seeking funds but am interested in hearing any concerns you have or suggestions for improvement."

There were murmurs of approval from the audience and some questions. One tall, bespectacled white haired man with a goatee stood up. "I have two granddaughters in Toronto and I can see myself urging my son to send them to your school. However, I have one concern. I know of other religious schools, both Jewish and Christian, that won't teach evolution and the early geological history of the Earth because of conflicts with the biblical story of Creation. What will you do?"

Good question, Ephraim thought, but Rebecca answered without a moment's hesitation. "There are two sides to the school — a religious side and a secular side. On the secular side, the standard curriculum set by Ontario will be followed, including evolutionary biology."

The goateed questioner was not satisfied. "What about the religious side? What will you teach there?"

Ephraim saw the look of stubbornness and anger spread across Rebecca's face. He jumped up. "Sir, with all due respect, it is a Jewish religious school we're talking about. We must teach the biblical story of Creation — some of us interpret the story as metaphorical while others lean towards a more literal view. Nevertheless, whatever our views, they won't intrude in the science classes."

"Are you involved in the school as well?" Joe asked.

"Yes. Rebecca has asked me to teach on both the religious and secular sides."

The goateed man did not seem entirely satisfied but he sat down. There was a round of applause as the meeting broke up.

Rebecca joined them for the trip back to Toronto. "I know you were trying to help me but I didn't like your answer."

They were both in the second row seats of the minivan. Dora was snoozing in the front passenger seat and Sholom was busy manoeuvring around the Sunday afternoon traffic.

"Rebecca, if you want your school to be a success, it must be perceived as balanced. It's not the ultra orthodox you want in your school. It's the children of moderate and non-observant Jews you need to attract if you want to preserve Judaism."

"Typical man. I offer you a subordinate role and already you're trying to take over."

He started to protest but saw the smile on her face and the large blue eyes staring gratefully at him. "Touché!" he said and they both laughed.

Sholom dropped Rebecca at Pearson International Airport where she had parked her car. "I can give you a lift," she said to Ephraim. "Rabbi Nitsky won't have to go all the way up to Steeles."

They chatted amicably as Rebecca drove him home. He leaned over and kissed her as he left the car and, once again, noticed that she made no objection to his touching her.

CHAPTER 4

At The Brink

He found a note on the kitchen table. "We are invited to the Feldmans for dinner," his mother wrote. "If you get home early enough, come over to the store and we can leave shortly after six."

The Feldmans lived further east, a good half hour away, in a gated apartment complex. He looked forward to seeing Alex again.

As he sauntered through the food court on his way to the store, he spotted a familiar figure sitting alone at a table. I should walk on, he told himself, nothing can come of this. But temptation was the stronger voice. Besides, she had seen him and was waving — ignoring her would be grossly impolite. He greeted Laura and sat down.

"What a nice surprise," she said. There was no mistaking the look of welcome and it reflected his own feelings of happiness at seeing her again. He heard the warning bells in his brain sounding incessantly but he was rooted to the chair, unable to tear himself away.

"You're having a coffee break," he stammered, appalled at the banality of the statement.

"Yes. Your mother insisted I take a break. I have to close tonight because the two of you are off to dinner. How did it go this weekend? Was your sermon well received? I'm sure you did well."

She had such an easy loquacious manner of speaking that, despite his excitement, he felt at ease. "What makes you think so?"

She pursed her lips in the impish way he found so charming. "If you were a priest, I'd come to church every Sunday."

He felt his face reddening. "You're a naughty girl. You're the kind of woman we religious types are trying to direct along the path of righteousness."

She giggled. "If you show me the path, I'll follow it."

The remark was meant to be repartee but had a quality of entreaty to it. Desire stabbed through him. He wanted to smash his lips against hers and hold her tightly. The warning bells now clanged continuously and blotted out the voices urging him on. She must have sensed the turmoil he was going through for she stopped smiling and glanced sadly away. She drained the last of the coffee in her cup and stood up. "I've got to get back to work."

He walked with her to the store and found it filled with customers. His mother gave him a quick nod. He went to the cash register and for the next hour was relieved to be busy. Just before six, he waited outside the store while his mother went off to the ladies room to freshen up. He watched Laura serving the final customers. He became aware that he was not alone. Frank Yanovich gave him a cursory nod but said nothing. What does a sweet young woman like Laura see in a brute like that? Ephraim thought.

The Feldmans were short and stocky and contrasted sharply with the taller, slimmer profiles of Marsha and Ephraim. Morris Feldman was a well-known criminal lawyer with an extensive practice in Ontario and throughout Canada. Esther did volunteer work with, and sat on the Boards of, a number of charities. Alex, the only child, still lived at home.

They occupied the penthouse of their building, a spacious apartment with an equally spacious patio that boasted a commanding view of the distant skyline of downtown Toronto. The mild spring weather allowed them and their guests to enjoy their drinks on the patio.

The two families had lived close to each other while Alex and Ephraim were growing up. The boys went through elementary and high school together. It was only during university that their paths had diverged.

Ephraim recounted his weekend experience in Guernsey, including the presentation given by Rebecca. Alex looked at him quizzically. "How did she end up in Guernsey the same time you were there?"

"Just coincidence," Ephraim answered, smiling.

Esther served dinner in a cosy eating area just off the main dining room. Their conversation never languished and touched on the mid-east situation, the similarities of common law to Talmudic law, and recent incidents of anti-Semitism in the Bathurst-Steeles neighbourhood.

Morris was indignant. "The three Chasidim who were beaten up were simply walking after the Maariv service along Bathurst, just south of Clarke, when they were set upon by a gang of thugs. The police insist it was a random event, not racially motivated. A detective friend tells me it smells of Eastern European anti-Semitism transported here. Anyway, random event or not, the police are stepping up their patrols. Marsha, perhaps you should consider moving out of the area. There are still some apartments available in this complex."

"Morris, I really like it where I live and besides, it's convenient to my store."

"I walk quite often in the area where the attack took place," Ephraim objected. "I've never seen anything threatening and I've never felt in any danger. Maybe the police are right and it was just an isolated incident by a bunch of guys who had nothing better to do."

After dinner, Morris, Esther and Marsha watched the CBC news while Alex and Ephraim took their drinks and sat outside on the patio. The air was cool but still comfortable and was buttressed by a patio heater that warmed and illuminated them.

"Something's bothering you, my friend," Alex observed. "Did the weekend not go well? Or was it the blonde dynamo."

Ephraim sniffed and tasted the brandy in his glass. "No, the weekend was a success and Rebecca was OK. But you're right. Something is bothering me."

Alex looked long and searchingly at his friend. "Is it anything I can help you with?"

"I don't think so. I think I'm in love. A girl."

"I'm glad it's a girl. Don't tell me you've fallen for the blonde bomber."

Ephraim shook his head. "I wish it were Rebecca, but as attractive as she is, it's someone else."

Alex put down his glass and leaned forward. "Is it somebody you met in Guernsey?"

"I had no end of attractive women lining up to meet me. You'd have been envious. But no, it's nobody in Guernsey. It's Laura Burton."

Alex stood up, his mouth hanging open in astonishment. "You're putting me on."

Ephraim sighed and shook his head. "I liked her the moment I met her. This afternoon, I saw her again in the food court at the mall. I stopped to talk to her. I almost came apart. Right now, I don't know what to do. I should just get her out of my mind and not go near the store. But I keep thinking about her and seeing her everywhere. I think she likes me too."

Alex began to pace up and down the patio. "In your present state, I shouldn't tell you this, but I know she likes you. She doesn't know we're friends. I overheard her talking to some of the other women at the Running Club. She was raving about her boss' son. At the time I thought — love's labour lost. But Freml, rabbis don't go after shiksas. You're heading into a mess if you don't stop now."

Ephraim tried hard to follow Alex's advice. He spent his days at the Chevra Kadisha Institute, his weekends in Guernsey, and made no attempt to visit the store or even the mall. True, he would glance surreptitiously around when he came out of the Clarke Street Synagogue or Solly's but never caught sight of Laura. Occasionally, he met with Rebecca to review his sermons or the prospectus she was preparing for the school. He tried to give himself up to her beauty, to lessen the hold Laura still had over him, but apart from stirring up his lust, he felt no compelling emotion. As time drifted through May and then June, he was convinced his desire for Laura was waning and her image was fading away. Once he was transferred to Nova Scotia, all thoughts of her, along with his infatuation, would end.

It was a request by his mother, responding to the imperatives of the store that shattered his resolve. Marsha announced at supper in early July that the following week she would attend the Atlanta Gift Show.

"I'm leaving next Saturday night and will be back late Thursday. Laura will run the store for the five days I'm away. Can you call in now and then just to make sure everything's going ok?"

He tried to demur. "Ma, I'm really busy at the Institute and working everyday with Sholom. I'm sure Laura can manage without my help."

Marsha was insistent. "Freml, all you have to do is call occasionally. You needn't go to the store unless something special is required. Laura has both our cell phone numbers. I can tell she's nervous about being in charge while I'm away so all she needs is some reassurance. I will also call in from time to time."

EPHRAIM

Ephraim was in Guernsey when Marsha left for Atlanta. As he drove back to Toronto on Sunday afternoon, he was disturbed by the excitement he felt as he contemplated calling Laura.

"Everything went well today," she reported. The initial cheery greeting turned flat and cold when she recognized the caller. "It was quiet today. I guess everybody's away."

"Well, it is July and a beautiful day." He was disappointed by the coldness of her tone — she didn't seem at all welcoming.

"I know you're very busy. I'll call you if I need any help."

"That sounds like — 'Don't call me, I'll call you.'"

There was a long pause. "It wasn't meant like that. Your mother explained — very proudly — that you were in Guernsey each weekend and had to prepare during the week. Plus you're getting ready to ship off to Nova Scotia. Also, your girlfriend was in one day and I heard her tell your mother that your sermons are excellent and you're helping her with her project — whatever that is. So it's obvious you're very busy and I don't want to add to your burden. Anyway, I've got to go now. A customer just came in and it's almost closing time."

He felt slapped down as he flicked his cell phone shut. Clearly she was angry with him. But why? True, he hadn't shown up at the store in over a month and another woman was reviewing his sermons. He thought back to their earlier encounters and realized that a bond of expectation had developed between them — a bond that he had deliberately quashed. For a moment, the idea that if Laura was jealous of Rebecca, there must be feeling for him roiled through him and challenged his determination not to have further contact. Yet, he thought, if she wants me to stay away, perhaps it's for the best. It makes it easier to forget her.

Nevertheless, he was troubled, alternatively congratulating himself on his exercise of will power and then sinking into a morass of longing for Laura. The turmoil continued even as he said the evening prayers and tried to focus on the sacred text.

"I know it's hard, but you're doing the right thing by staying away," Alex reassured him. They were sitting in the lobby bar of the Royal York Hotel later that Sunday night. Alex had invited Ephraim to meet Polly Macrae, his new girl friend, — "this one's serious" — an opera singer, and they were waiting for her to show up.

"Alex, you're kind of hypocritical. You want me to keep clear of Laura because she's not Jewish, but you're quite happy — even eager — to introduce me to your girlfriend who isn't Jewish."

Alex poured some water into his Scotch and took a hefty swallow. "True, Polly was brought up as a Protestant but one of her grandmothers was Jewish. Anyway, I'm not a rabbi about to start my career. If you get involved with Laura, you can say goodbye to your career. Have you talked about it with your mother?"

Ephraim shook his head. "No, not yet. I'm not sure what her reaction would be and it might affect Laura's employment. I've just got to forget her."

Alex nodded and stood up as a woman approached their table. Polly was a few inches taller than Alex and had to bend slightly as she and Alex embraced and kissed.

"Oh, I'm so happy tonight," Polly gushed after the introduction to Ephraim. "I received an extra vigorous round of applause at the curtain bows. Hope I'm not too late. It took forever to get the makeup off and there were people to say hello to. I ran like mad the few blocks from the Opera House."

She was dressed in white t-shirt and slacks. Straight black hair framed a somewhat pale but attractive face. She ordered a beer and immediately downed half of it.

"Opera is such thirsty work," she said.

"Polly was Musetta in La Bohème tonight," Alex explained, fondly stroking her hair.

"It's an opera I love to sing in. The Bohemian life. So free, so unregimented, souls devoted to art and love, asking nothing more than occasional good fortune, enough to buy a baguette and a bottle of wine, no questions asked, inside yet outside the establishment. But I think I'm preaching to the wrong person. Alex tells me you're a rabbi. I suppose you frown on Bohemian life."

"Not necessarily. As long as the bottle of wine and the baguette are kosher, the Bohemians observe the Sabbath, and their relationships are sanctified by marriage, then Bohemian life would be quite acceptable."

After they had stopped laughing, Alex said very seriously, "I bet Ephraim would like to be a Bohemian now."

Yes, Ephraim thought, and then I would have no qualms about whom to love. He explained his dilemma to Polly.

EPHRAIM

"I don't know enough to advise," Polly said. "Alex and I have the same problem. I'm going to meet his parents soon, and Alex has warned me it will be difficult but they'll accept me. I expect my parents will be disappointed at first but Alex is so likeable, they'll come around. People on either side of the divide seem to have trouble when their children decide to cross the line."

Ephraim leaned forward and looked at them glumly. "In my case, I'm not yet worried about parent reaction. Rabbis aren't supposed to even get near the line."

Polly nodded sympathetically and ran her fingers through Alex's hair. "I'm glad you're not a rabbi, Alex. We just have parents to face."

"Yeah, no big deal. However, we won't meet my parents on the patio. It's a long fall from the penthouse floor."

The turmoil didn't leave Ephraim as he returned home and slept restlessly that night. At the Chevra Kadisha Institute, he finally got control of his emotions as he studied intensely the work of Maimonides. He felt himself at ease once again when his cell phone rang.

"I'm afraid I have to ask for your help after all." Laura's voice was welcoming, even gracious. "One of our best customers was in and ordered a full dinner set for eight of the Lomonozov cable pattern. Between what we have in the stockroom and on display, I can put together his order. But he wants it delivered this afternoon. It's a $2,000 sale."

Ephraim was on fire, sweating profusely at the thought of seeing her once again. He would have gone immediately except he realized he had to calm down. He managed to stammer out that he'd be there after lunch.

He forced himself to eat the cottage cheese salad that Dora had prepared and declined the tea and cookies. He picked the Cadillac up at the apartment and drove to the mall. Laura smiled as he entered the store and greeted him with her usual cheery manner. He relished the warmth of her greeting and the sparkle in her eyes. There were two other saleswomen in the store who nodded to him.

"We'll go to the stockroom first and bring up what we have there."

He pushed the four-wheeled platform truck ahead as they walked through the mall to the stockroom a good distance away. Laura bubbled with excitement as she told him about the sale and how happy Marsha would be.

"The customer came in for a hostess gift and while I was wrapping it, he mentioned that he was going to Holt's or Ashley's to buy a set of dinner dishes. I showed him the Lomonozov — the cable pattern — and told him the story — that the pattern dates back to Catherine the Great and has been recently produced again in a restored St. Petersburg pottery. I showed him the picture of Gorbachev drinking from a cable pattern teacup. Then I cleared one of the tables and showed him what a place setting would look like."

Ephraim tried to listen but her voice came to him like light through fog. He glanced at her beside him, her hands gesticulating as she recounted the triumph of her sale, her eyes wide in excitement, her lips racing to form the words, her whole body incredibly alive.

She unlocked the stockroom door and they stepped inside. Shelving stretched around the perimeter of the room and the centre was piled high with boxes.

"All the Lomonozov is in the centre. It'll take a couple of trips to get it all to the store. I'll help you with the first load."

She stepped to the pile but he remained rooted to the spot, unable to move, completely enraptured by the sight of her body twisting to the boxes, her arms raised emphasizing the curvature of her breasts, her skirt rising up to reveal a knee and a patch of thigh.

She turned back to him. "You're not listening to me." She frowned but there was a smile on the pouting lips.

No signal occurred, no invitation, no reaching out a tentative hand — but suddenly, they were in each others arms, bodies entwined, lips pressed against lips. Her feet dangled a few inches off the ground as Ephraim straightened up, still clasping her, one hand moving up and down her back, from the nape of the neck to the round firm buttocks. Their lips pushed open and their tongues bored into each other's mouth, caressing and exploring. They stopped kissing but stood embraced, breathing hard. Ephraim's mouth and nose buried in her hair.

After a few minutes, she slowly pushed away from him. She took his hand and kissed it. "Let's do the delivery and talk later."

He threw himself into the work with such enthusiasm that she had to remind him of the fragile nature of porcelain. He was ecstatic — he loved a woman and his love had been returned. He floated along on a bubble of erotic emotion. Occasionally, the thought that either their love or his rabbinic career would not survive threatened to burst the bubble but he pushed the thought aside. Surely, the happiness he felt could not be wrong and would persevere.

He glanced at Laura walking beside him as he pushed the platform truck loaded with boxes back to the store. "I love you," he said to her.

She smiled up at him. "I hope so. Otherwise I'll have to complain to your mother about sexual harassment."

The car was fully loaded as they set off for the customer's house a half-hour drive away. The carefully packed Lomonozov order jammed the trunk and back seat of the Cadillac. Laura insisted on joining him for the delivery and sat beside him with the final box on her lap.

"Why did you not come to the store for over a month?" Laura demanded, tearfully.

Ephraim wheeled the car out of the mall, and turned north on Bathurst Street. "I tried very hard to forget you and staying away was the only way I knew how."

"But why?"

He stopped at a red light. He reached out a hand and combed his fingers through her hair.

"Because you're not Jewish and rabbis are not supposed to get involved with non-Jewish girls. Besides, you have a boyfriend."

"I broke it off with Frank a few weeks ago. What about your girlfriend?"

He eased the car east onto the Electronic Toll Highway that girds the top of Toronto and accelerated to the speed limit. "Rebecca is not my girlfriend. She's a friend of the family. She's planning to open a school and I'm helping her with the project. She also wants me to teach at the school. Did you break off with Frank because of me?"

There was a long pause. "Partly. But there's another reason. Frank asked me to do something that I found very shocking. He wanted me to quit my job. He said I shouldn't work for Jews. 'We fixed them in Russia,' he says. 'We got this guy Khordovsky in jail and others have been kicked out. Canada will get smart one of these days and get rid of them here.' I told him to knock such silly ideas out of his head. In Canada, we all live happily together. But he got angrier and angrier and I sent him packing."

They drove in silence for a few moments. "What about us?" she asked. "Do we have a future together, despite our religious differences?"

Yes, that's the real question, Ephraim thought. Perhaps the only question. He mulled over the question and took too long to answer.

"Then why did you kiss me and say you loved me?" she snapped.

He exited the highway at Leslie Street and stopped at a red light. "I kissed you because I love you and right now I can't see a life without you." He cradled her chin in his hand and turned her head towards him. "If I hesitate, it's because I'm wrestling with how to pull it off. Even a Jewish girl would find life with a rabbi difficult. There are so many rules and regulations to follow, starting with keeping an absolutely kosher home. My fear is — once you see what's required of you, you'll send me packing like Frank."

She grasped his hand, thrust two of his fingers into her mouth, and chewed on them.

"Ow!"

She released his fingers. "I just wanted to taste kosher food."

A horn honked behind him. He quickly retrieved his hand, drove the remaining few blocks and parked in front of the customer's home.

It was a large house, almost entirely covering its piece of land. The street was filled with similar homes, many boasting three car garages.

"Quite a place," Ephraim said.

"Yes, " Laura agreed and put a mock serious look on her face. "Some men take care of their wives."

Ephraim in turn looked serious. "Your customer must be earning more than a rabbi's salary."

She reached up and fondled his face. "A smaller house will do me fine. What's more important is who's there with me. Now, how about getting this heavy box off me."

An Asian woman opened the door. In broken English, she invited them into a large entrance hallway and told them her husband would be back shortly. They stacked the boxes in the hallway. Laura insisted on unpacking and helping to put the dishes away. The customer arrived — also Asian — as they were finishing and obviously pleased, bowed and shook their hands.

On the way back to the store, Ephraim stopped at a strip mall near the highway. They leaned over the narrow gap between the seats, embraced and kissed.

"There's a Tim Horton's," Laura noted. "The Zimmerman family owes me a coffee for my fine work."

They sat beside each other in the coffee shop. Laura had ordered a doughnut as well.

"Why aren't you having a doughnut?"

Ephraim put an arm around her waist and pulled her tightly to him. "I can't be sure it's kosher. I don't know what oil it was fried in or what else was fried in the pan."

She put the doughnut down. "I guess there are many things I'll have to learn. Does it offend you if I eat the doughnut?"

He nuzzled her hair with his mouth and kissed her cheek. "Nothing you do can offend me."

They returned to the Esplanade and sat in the car, holding hands.

"I really should get back to the store," Laura said. "I'd like to make sure everything's ok before I go home."

He nodded but didn't release her hand. "What happens now?" she asked. "Can we tell the world we're in love?".

Can we? he asked himself. Deep down he felt a sense of shame — he was transgressing a basic tenet of his religious beliefs. What would his mother, his family, Sholom Nitsky think? What synagogue would hire a rabbi who intermarried? He would be looked upon as renegade, lapsed, unable to challenge temptation. On the other hand, his love for this woman engrossed him entirely, pushed away all thought except the desire to hold her, to possess her, to make her his wife. He felt so much at peace with Laura sitting beside him. Surely, a just God could not consider such feelings as evil. Yet, sadly, he knew there would be many problems that would have to be faced and resolved.

"Let's keep it quiet for now. I'd like to find out how to protect my career and not give you up. And you have your family to contend with. Your mother may also have a problem with intermarriage."

She threw her arms around his neck and laughed. "Are you asking me to marry you? We've only just kissed. First you have to court me."

He kissed her eyes shut. "Fine, let's start tonight. Evening prayers should be finished a little after nine o'clock. I'll pick you up around 9:30 and we'll go for a drink."

His cell phone was vibrating as he left the Clarke Street Synagogue and walked quickly to the Cadillac parked a short distance away. "Ephraim, sweetheart, let's not meet tonight," Laura said, her voice subdued. "I didn't tell my mother how we feel about each other but I did tell her how you helped me today and what a fine guy you are. I guess I went overboard. She saw right through me and got very upset. We had a long talk about how these intermarriages don't work. Would I have to give up my religion?"

There were too many people around. "Hang on while I get into the car." His fingers shook as he manipulated the remote control to open the door. Was his world already falling apart? "Ok, I can talk now. I'm not sure about the answer to your question. I suspect that if I'm to continue as a rabbi, you'd have to convert."

There was a long pause. "Ephraim, I'm not very religious as I told you but I do believe in Jesus and I pray to Him in my own way. Even if I convert, I wouldn't want to give up Jesus."

"Sweetheart, I don't want you to give up anything that will make you unhappy. It's true that Jews don't accept Jesus as divine and a messiah. We're not even as generous as the Moslems who accept Him as a prophet. We identify Him with 2,000 years of persecution. What it might mean if you convert is you couldn't profess openly your belief in Jesus, especially not as a rabbi's wife. It would just be something between us."

There was another long pause. "My mother's upset because being Catholic preserves my father's memory and the family tradition which goes way back. She says our children — her grandchildren — would no longer be Catholic."

"I suppose your mother is right. My mother will say the same thing if the children are Catholic. As a rabbi, I'd have to insist that the children be raised Jewish. Does this bother you very much?"

"Right now I don't know. All I can think of is you. But it does bother me that we all assume I will have to give up my religion for yours. If we truly love each other, why do we have to give up anything?" She was crying now, her voice breaking. "I've got to say goodbye now. My mother's knocking on my door. Call you later."

He drove slowly back to the apartment, unmindful of the motorists who honked impatiently behind him and then turned out past him with a screech of tires and invective. He'd visualized a picture of him and Laura, alone in a gondola hanging from a balloon, floating blissfully around the world. Now, the balloon was on fire and they were in free fall back to earth.

He sat in the living room, unread newspapers on his lap, pondering the situation. Alex had warned him he was heading for a mess but he could no more turn off his feelings for Laura than try to stop the wind. He knew Mrs. Burton's reaction was a harbinger of things to come, that people close to him — like his mother — would be dismayed by his choice. And yet what kind of world was it that frowned on the love of two lovers? His intentions were honourable. If their love prospered, as he truly believed, he would marry Laura. Why could he not practice as a rabbi and she remain Catholic? Sure, she'd have to learn how to keep a kosher home but that was relatively easy. And so what if she stayed Catholic? He wasn't an evangelist trying to convert the world.

The ringing of his cell phone jarred him loose from his gloom. Without looking at the display, he flicked open the phone and spoke softly into the mouthpiece: "Hi, sweetheart."

There was silence at the other end and then a voice snapped. "It's your cousin Gertie. Does Irving know how you feel about me or were you expecting somebody else?"

Gertie's voice brought him firmly back to reality. Sarcasm was required to hide his confusion. "It's the latest in rabbinical greetings. We're supposed to be cool."

"I hope it was Rebecca you were expecting. She called around six all in a panic. She'd been trying all afternoon to invite you to a meeting tonight regarding her school. She thinks you've fainted somewhere — apparently you have a problem with too much coffee. I've been calling you as well. Are you ok?"

"Of course, I'm ok. I guess my cell phone was turned off. I had to help out at the store today. A big sale required a big delivery."

"Well, call Rebecca. She must be home by now."

Rebecca kept him on the line longer than he wished as she described excitedly and at length her meeting with the Canadian Jewish Weekly. "I hope the interview will bring lots of interest. I gave you as an example of the young, well-educated teachers eager to be part of the school and capable of teaching on both the religious and secular sides. Do you mind?"

No, he didn't mind. All he wanted was to end the conversation tactfully and to keep the line open for Laura's call. Finally, they wished each other good night and agreed to meet in two days at the Bathurst Jewish Community Services. "If you come around 5:30, I'll be finished with my summer class and we can find a conference room in which to work."

He checked his cell phone and the land line — no messages from Laura.

He mumbled through the Night Prayer unable to concentrate on the text or its meaning. He felt a deep sense of loss, like bereavement, and had to remind himself that they had only declared their love for each other that afternoon. He debated whether to call her, but it was already very late, and suppose her mother answered. What would he say? "Hello, I'm the man who's causing the problem." Perhaps, it was wise they go no further.

He crawled into bed and glanced through the newspaper, trying to get his mind off Laura. Towards midnight, he dozed off into a restless, fitful sleep. He awoke abruptly to the sound of the cell phone ringing on the night table.

"Did I wake you up?" a soft, sultry voice beguiled him, banishing all his gloomy thoughts.

"I'm glad you called. When I didn't hear from you, I thought it was all over."

She laughed. "You won't get rid of me that quickly. My mother and I had a long talk and a good cry. Women do that. We didn't fix the problem, but our relationship is still very strong. We were always very close but when my father died, we became even closer. My mother has to be part of us."

"Should I meet her?"

"No, not yet. She only knows how I feel about you. She doesn't know how you feel about me. She's worried that I'll go after you and how could you resist her daughter?"

"She's absolutely right. Look what happened."

Her delicious laughter sounded in his ear. He turned on a side, pressing the cell phone into the pillow and hard up against his face. "I love you. You can come with anyone you like, your mother especially — even Jesus."

She laughed even harder. They agreed to meet for lunch the next day in the Esplanade. Ephraim was giddy with happiness and desire as he said goodnight and slowly drifted off, still lying on the cell phone.

CHAPTER 5

Elijah Is Not Happy

Something prodded him awake. Startled, he sat up blinking, dazzled by the golden haze that lit up the room. The tall robed figure of Elijah stood beside the bed.

"Do not be afraid. I come to have discourse with you."

Ephraim pulled out the chair and helped Elijah to sit down. He climbed back into the bed and stared uneasily at the prophet. Elijah looked grim.

"In our last conversation, I commanded you to bolster your faith and to eliminate your doubts. Not only have you failed to do so, you are careening perilously close to the infernal regions of Baal."

Fearful, Ephraim asked humbly: "What do you mean? I worship only one God, the God of Israel."

Elijah snapped angrily: "For the sake of a woman, you will allow other gods into your household. In your heart you are prepared to desert Israel for this woman who is not of any of our tribes."

Ephraim reached out to the prophet beseechingly. "Eliyahu, I love her. I cannot live without her. She is a good woman. She returns my love. Surely, the Lord will understand and forgive."

Elijah shook his head, a pitying look in his eyes. "You are deceived like Samson was deceived by Delilah. All his strength was as nothing compared to the wiles of a woman. You are caught by the same snare. Follow the example of our revered father Abraham and cast your Hagar from your midst. Wed the Israelite — she will satisfy your carnal impulses and bring fulfillment to your house. In time you will forget the other."

Ephraim started to say that he had tried and it hadn't worked but the darkness in the room told him Elijah was gone. He fell back onto the pillow, into a brief instant of remorse and guilt until the blackness of sleep claimed him.

"Ephraim, I don't think you're listening to me," Sholom Nitsky said gently, a frown indicating his irritation. "It's important that we talk about the communities you'll be visiting in the field. Are you losing interest?"

Ephraim and Sholom were sitting at the small conference table in Sholom's office. A road map of Nova Scotia covered the table. Sholom had circled dots on the map and was describing the people Ephraim would meet. Ephraim was to take notes but his pen had stopped moving on the pad before him.

"I'm sorry," Ephraim reassured him. "I'm still very interested. I had a restless night and I'm finding it difficult to concentrate."

Sholom looked at him worriedly. "It's already after ten. Let's get some coffee in the kitchen."

Ephraim had awakened early that morning, fatigued and uneasy. He pursued the Morning Prayer with intense energy and devotion, trying to pour his anguish and uncertainty into the sacred words. He repeated several times the clarion call of Jewry from time immemorial: "Hear, O Israel, the Lord is our God, the Lord is One." How could anyone — Elijah, or for that matter, the Almighty — doubt his loyalty and conviction? His love for Laura had not changed his commitment to Judaism, or his passion for his career. Surely she could bring into the marriage ideas that were dear to her — they were like keepsakes from an earlier time. His mother still had a large soft bear prominently displayed in her bedroom that his father had won for her when they were honeymooning at Coney Island. No one accused her of idolatry. But even as he thought this, he recognized the futility of the comparison. While he might denigrate the stature of the Christian Messiah, his fellow Jews and the world at large would agree there was a profound difference between a teddy bear and Jesus.

Sholom filled the cups and carried them back to his office. "What kept you awake last night? Are you worried about your mission?"

Ephraim poured milk into his coffee. "No, not really. There's a problem I'm wrestling with. Perhaps you can help me think it through."

Sholom nodded and folded up the map of Nova Scotia. They drank their coffee in silence for a few moments.

EPHRAIM

"A friend of mine — a very good friend — " Ephraim began hesitantly, "wants to marry a non-Jewish woman. He hasn't said so, but I believe he will ask me to officiate. What should I tell him?"

Sholom nodded and pensively stroked his beard. "Unfortunately, it's not an unusual problem these days. You'll find intermarriage fairly common, particularly in communities with small Jewish populations. At one time, a rabbi had no choice but to refuse to marry the couple. However, now we're bowing to reality. I'll accept to officiate provided the non-Jewish partner converts and the conversion is serious. This means he or she must study our religion, accept it, and agree to bring up the children as Jews."

"Do you judge whether the convert is serious? I thought there are Beit Din."

Sholom nodded. "You're right. There are Beit Din in Montreal and in quite a few cities in the US. The court decides and they're pretty tough. It's not a rubber stamp exercise. The convert really has to be serious so advise your friend if his fiancée agrees to take this route, it's for real."

"OK, but how do they decide if someone is serious?"

Sholom carefully set his coffee cup down. "Sometimes determining somebody is not serious is very simple. The convert admits he or she will still celebrate Christmas, not because it's a religious thing but it's tied up with family and childhood memories. A lot of the decision is based on the judges' questioning of the convert's sincerity, knowledge of Jewish law and ritual, and likelihood to carry out the responsibilities and obligations of a Jew. I've participated in a Beit Din — let me tell you, it's no easy task."

Still rankling from his brush with Elijah and bolstered by his talk with Sholom, Ephraim went to his lunch date with Laura, fully resolved to insist on her full conversion, no Christian remnants attached, if their love was to proceed. Then he saw her walking towards him, the pouting lips wreathed in a broad smile, eyes sparkling, hips swaying slightly, well-formed knees and legs striding prominently below her short, tight skirt. In that brief moment before they embraced and kissed, he understood profoundly why Jacob had indentured himself for fourteen years for Rebecca, why David had let nothing stand in his way to possess Bathsheba and why Samson gave his strength away to Delilah. As Ephraim stood there holding Laura hard against him, he felt his resolve melt away, replaced by passion and desire, all thought of consequences suppressed.

"If you still want to keep our feelings secret," she whispered in his ear, giggling, "kissing in a food court at lunchtime is no way."

They broke apart and looked around embarrassedly. No one seemed to be paying any attention.

"You have to teach me how to eat kosher," Laura said. "I'll eat whatever you do."

He looked around the food court. There was the usual collection of fast food outlets. "The only place I can get something kosher to eat is Tim Horton's. A tomato and lettuce on a sandwich bun should be ok."

They ordered the sandwiches with coffee and found a table off to one side. "Before we eat, I have to say grace," he informed her and said the prayer blessing the bread.

"That was short and sweet," Laura said. "What does it mean?"

"Blessed art Thou, O Lord, King of the Universe, Who has brought forth bread from out of the earth."

Laura bit into her sandwich. "It's similar to our Catholic grace but we bless the Lord for all the food, not just the bread."

They chewed away on their sandwiches, occasionally sipping their coffees. "Bread and wine are symbolic with us just as they are for Christians. Your Christ must have made the same blessing over the bread at the famous Last Supper just as I did now."

She laughed. "I hope this is not our Last Lunch. Now, start telling me what I have to know about your religion. What makes something kosher?"

He sensed her seriousness and felt relieved that perhaps she would accommodate him and convert. They spent the remainder of the lunch hour discussing the fundamentals of Judaism.

"A life without bacon," Laura marvelled as they were leaving the food court. "I guess if our priest can give up sex for religion, I can give up pork."

He kissed her lips, the tip of her nose, her forehead. "We do have sex," he said, chuckling. "I promise you lots of it. Can we have lunch again tomorrow? I'll bring the lunch."

"That sounds wonderful. What about dinner tomorrow night? I'm off at six. Tonight I have to close at nine."

He shook his head. "No, I promised Rebecca I'd meet her at five o'clock and work on her prospectus. I don't know how long it will take and then I have the Evening Prayers starting around eight."

They were walking side by side. Laura stopped short and grasped his elbow. "Do you mean after all the nice things you said to me, you're going out with another woman?"

"Please don't be upset. I'm involved in her school project and we'll meet regularly as the project gets going. I expect to teach in her school. I love you and only you."

She folded her arms akimbo and gave him a stern look. "OK, but that girl has her eyes on you. It was pretty apparent when she popped into the store and was talking to your mother about you. After she was gone, your mother explained that your family would like to see the two of you together."

"Laura, it takes two to tango. I want to dance my life away with you and no one else. I believe my mother is neutral on whom I marry. It's one of my uncles who's pushing the match and he's been told to mind his own business."

Her delicious laughter inflamed him. "In addition to the Jewish religion, I have to learn to tango. I'll meet you at your car at the Clarke Street Synagogue after I close the store tonight and you can take me out as you promised."

Ephraim returned to the Chevra Kadisha Institute for his afternoon session and was cheerful and focussed and filled his notebook with Sholom's comments.

"I see our little talk this morning has helped you," Sholom observed.

Ephraim paused in his note taking. "Yes. I passed on your advice and my friend reports he has every confidence his girlfriend will convert."

It bothered Ephraim that he was not entirely truthful with Sholom and was not at all certain that Sholom's advice would apply to a rabbi. If Laura became seriously involved in the conversion process, he would reveal all to Sholom and Dora. Doubtless, they would be disappointed but by then, he would be immersed in his work in Nova Scotia and good reports from the field would weigh in his favour.

But Sholom and Dora were not the only ones that needed to be told. The idea of conversion had already caused Laura's mother to react negatively. He dreaded the domestic storm that would erupt with his own family even if Laura converted. And his involvement in Rebecca's school would come to an abrupt halt — of that, he was sure. These anxieties weighed heavily on him but they blew away when an image of Laura popped into his mind — her smile, pouting lips, clear sparkling eyes, the hour-glass figure, and the charm of her forthright speech and easy manner. Would he not sacrifice all for her?

They sat side by side on a sofa bench running along the back wall of a small bar on Eglinton Avenue. He and Alex used to frequent the bar before Ephraim went off to Yeshiva University. In the semi-darkness, they embraced and kissed, nursed their drinks and occasionally got up to dance on the small dance floor. The music was too loud for ordinary speech so they mouthed their messages of love into each others' ears.

"What will you tell your mother?" Ephraim asked as he drove Laura home.

"She knows we're having a drink together. I told her when I called to say I wouldn't be home after work. Ephraim, I can't lie to her. We're more like sisters. I haven't told her how we feel about each other but she knows — she can see right through me. I'm so happy these days — I can't hide it. Even Thelma — the other regular sales girl at the store — made a comment like 'something's happened in your life.' What about your mother? When will you tell her?"

He parked the car in front of her apartment building on Hilda. "I don't know. My inclination is to keep us secret for a while. My mother will be shocked, as will the whole Zimmerman family. If my mother reacts badly, you may lose your job. When my boss finds out, he might very well dump me. Two unemployed people starting out in life is not a good thing."

She looked at him in surprise. "It never occurred to me that your mother would fire me. We get along so well — she's like a favourite aunt. I want her to love me. Surely, she will realize how strong our feelings are and accept me just as I know my mother will accept you."

He leaned over and kissed her. "A lot depends on how we present our case, both for my job and my mother. If it's obvious you're studying Judaism with the intention of converting, then we may get acceptance."

She frowned. "We seem to be worrying more about your family and your career than mine. Of course, I want to learn about the religion that's important to you, so that I don't offend you or your family in any way. But I haven't decided to convert because that would make my mother very unhappy."

"Laura, sweetheart, I don't want to make anyone unhappy, least of all you. I'm merely suggesting conversion as a way out of the mess." He knew it was the wrong way to put it the moment he uttered the words.

Angrily, she turned on him. "Mess? Is that what our love is? I know a better way to avoid the mess." She threw the door open, sprang from the car and disappeared into the building.

He ran into the building after her. He found the Burton name on the list of tenants but then decided not to ring. It was close to midnight and he would wake her mother and have two angry women to placate. Their love affair had lasted two days and like the warmth of an early spring had vanished with the first storm.

For the second night in a row, he sat disconsolately in the living room, unread newspapers spilling off his lap onto the floor. He tried watching television but could not concentrate and soon turned it off.

He started to say the Night Prayer but found the opening words wooden in his mouth, unable even to complete the first 'Hear, O Israel…' When you're in trouble, you're supposed to appeal to God, he thought. When his father had died, his prayers had been fervent and had helped him cope with the tragedy and gave him the support he needed to comfort his mother. Losing Laura was far less a disaster — let's face it, a mere setback in life — yet he found himself unable to seek succour in prayer. Was he blaming God? Was it God's will that he and Laura break up? After all, Ephraim was fully aware of the fundamental rules that governed his religion, but his statements and thoughts implied that he was prepared to break them. Elijah had warned him. Now was Ephraim's chance to avoid a situation that boded ill for everyone. However, he wanted no lingering bad feelings between him and Laura. He resolved to call her in the morning, explain that their relationship was indeed a mess, and that it was best for both of them to call a halt. With that, still sitting in the sofa chair, he dozed off.

The ringing of his cell phone woke him. Still groggy, he felt the stiffness in his neck and arm as he reached for the phone on the side table, nearly knocking over the lamp. The mantle clock indicated 2:30.

Her voice was flat and cold. "I hope I woke you. I can't sleep and I don't see why you should."

Elation flowed through him. "I haven't gone to bed yet. I was going to call you in the morning and explain what I meant."

"What is there to explain? I understand the word 'mess.'"

He cursed himself for being so stupid. "Laura, I don't care what word I used or what I was trying to say — I love you, madly, completely, no strings attached."

There was a long pause. He knew she was crying because he could hear the sniffling sounds. "If I don't convert, will you be able to practice as a rabbi?"

"I don't think so. Maybe I could get work as a teacher in the Public School System or get a doctorate and teach in a university."

"Do you want to practice as a rabbi?"

"Yes, but if I have to choose between my career and you, it's you I will pick. I can't bear to lose you."

Her voice was easier now, even seductive. "Maybe I'll love you again after all. Are we still on for lunch tomorrow?"

"Later on today," he reminded her.

"Are you going to sleep now?" she asked

"I'll say the Night Prayer first and then hit the sack. Will you be able to sleep now?"

"First I want to listen to the Night Prayer. If I'm going to be a rabbi's wife, I'd better start learning right away. Do you pray in English or Hebrew?"

"Normally Hebrew but tonight I'll read it to you in English." The prayer takes ten minutes to recite. He thought she'd fall asleep but she thanked him when he finished and wished him goodnight.

Ecstatic, he found himself bursting with happiness over their rekindled love. He strode up and down the living room. He kicked off his shoes, tore off his shirt and stepped out of his trousers, flung his underwear and socks across the room, and naked, stood there giggling. "It's a good thing, you're not here, Ma," he said out loud. "You'd lock me away."

Recalling his mother sobered him immediately. Soon he would have to tell her and he dreaded the moment. She would not be pleased with his choice of wife. He picked up his clothing, went to his bedroom and crawled into bed.

As the darkness of sleep overpowered him, a golden haze illuminated the room. Elijah stood looking mournfully at him, slowly shaking his head from side to side.

"Eliyahu," Ephraim cried out. "I tried. I cannot live without her. The moment I see her, the moment I hear her voice, or even think about her, I want her. Nothing else matters. You must understand how I feel."

The prophet continued to solemnly shake his head. "What is there to understand? You will have her at any cost? Is that what I am to understand? To satisfy your carnal impulse, you are prepared to repudiate the Almighty's commandments, to desecrate His Torah. Is the woman a storm of wind that she sweeps you before her like chaff? The Israelite woman awaits you — seize her before it is too late."

Ephraim shrank before the stern gaze of the prophet. "Eliyahu, I cannot. Please forgive me. She will become Jewish, she will be my rebbetsyn, our children will be Jewish. She will be a ger tzedek."

"And if she refuses?"

Ephraim hung his head in despair.

The prophet reached out and laid a hand on Ephraim's head. "My child, I fear for you. You are embarking on a dangerous journey. May the one God shine his countenance upon you and protect you."

The golden haze slowly evaporated and Elijah disappeared.

As promised, Ephraim had prepared the lunch —chicken and lettuce between slices of white bread smeared with salad dressing, and a couple of apples. "We can drink coffee or tea but it must be without milk or cream." He explained the dietary rules and the rigid separation between meat and dairy foods. "It extends even to dishes. In the kosher home, there are always two sets of dishes — one for meat and poultry meals and the other for meals where fish and dairy products are eaten."

"Wonderful," Laura said. "That means I'll start off with two sets of dishes."

Chuckling, he noted, "My mother has two every day sets, two sets for more formal occasions, and two sets for the eight-day Passover period and that's pretty typical.

"Six sets of dishes," Laura exclaimed. "My mother will think I've struck it rich. I think I'll go to Russia and Germany for the dishes. They have such beautiful porcelain."

He reached across the table, and stroked her cheek. "On a rabbi's salary, we'll start off at Wal-Mart, and maybe The Bay."

They were sitting in the food court at The Esplanade, oblivious to the lunchtime crowd that surrounded them. They drank black coffee as they slowly ate the sandwich lunch. After the problems of the previous night, they were light hearted, even giddy, whispering their love to each other, joking and teasing each other as lovers do.

"I've got to go back to work," Laura said, standing up. "I know you're busy with my rival at five o'clock, but can we meet at nine again? That was so nice last night. I promise not to get angry with you, no matter what you say."

He walked around the table and kissed her on the lips. "See you at nine. I promise not to say anything stupid." He watched her walk back to the store, almost maddened by the sight of the swaying hips, the purposeful stride displaying the shapely legs.

"You're in a good mood," Rebecca observed as Ephraim met her in the reception lobby of the Community Centre. Before she could object, he grasped her hand and kissed her on both cheeks.

She frowned and drew back. "Ephraim, today I am not clean."

Laughing, he dropped her hand. "Then you should wear a sign on these days or at least give me a calendar marked with the days I cannot touch you."

His mood was infectious. Rebecca relaxed and smiled broadly. "You're a naughty man. I don't know how they let you graduate at Yeshiva U. Before I hire you, I'll have to examine your certificate to make sure it's not a forgery."

"It is," he nodded sombrely. "Made it myself with a computer and a Xerox machine."

She looked at him in horror. "Ephraim, you can't be serious."

"Of course, I'm not serious. C'mon. Let's get to work. What and where?"

She led him down a long hallway into a room near the back of the building. A rather dishevelled looking man rose as they entered and presented a card to Ephraim.

"Brian Ruby is a reporter with The Canadian Jewish Weekly," Rebecca explained. "He's writing a story about my school and would like to interview you. He's already interviewed some of the other teachers who are interested in participating. Do you mind?"

No, I don't mind, he thought, but I wish you would've told me. Aloud he said, "Sounds wonderful. I'll be a good subject, Mr. Ruby. As a rabbi, I have to tell the truth."

Brian Ruby twisted his lips into a sardonic sneer, pointed to a chair opposite him and took out a recording device and a notepad from his briefcase. His dirty white T-shirt emblazoned with the word PRESS in red letters hung loosely on him. His khaki slacks looked like he'd slept in them. He rubbed bony fingers over his stubbled chin and cheeks and pushed a button on the recorder. Rebecca sat down beside him.

"Rebecca has told me all about you," Brian began, his voice low and raspy.

Ephraim had taken an instant dislike to him. "Well, then, we don't need the interview."

"Nah, she's told me all the external things about you. I want to go deeper. You don't look like a rabbi. I can't even see whether your head is covered." He stood up and walked behind Ephraim. "Yeah, you got your beanie on. You look more like a movie star."

"Mr. Ruby," Rebecca objected, "can we not get on with the interview? Rabbi Zimmerman is a very busy man."

Brian Ruby sat down again and poised pencil over notepad. "OK. Why are you interested in the school?" As he asked the question, he raked his eyes towards Rebecca sitting beside him.

Ephraim bristled but decided to take the question seriously. "I'm interested in all things Jewish and in new ways to teach Judaism. Miss Zifkin makes a very compelling case for her school. She has the drive, the ambition and the personality to pull it off. It's exciting to be part of such a project."

There was a pause as Brian scribbled a few notes. "Yeah, yeah. You all say that. You all sound like you're reading off the same page. There are lots of parochial schools in Toronto — why this one?"

"I checked out some of the others. This is the only one with a Miss Rebecca Zifkin as its head. Also the idea of teaching secular subjects in Hebrew as well as English got me interested."

Rebecca stood up. "This is going to my head. Why don't the two of you continue and I'll be back shortly."

Ephraim waited until she left the room. "You think I'm interested in the school because of her, don't you?"

"Why not?" Brian shrugged. "With an ass and tits like that, who wouldn't be interested? Don't tell me you're not into her yet."

Ephraim shook his head in wonder. "What rock did you crawl out from? What kind of reporter are you? How could the CJW hire you?"

"I'm a freelancer. I'm just doing this to get started in my journalism career."

"Well, you're obviously a future Pulitzer-prize candidate. What else would you like to know about me?"

Brian stood up and leaned over the table. "Don't get sarcastic with me. You know, depending on how I write this story, I could crumble the school before it even starts."

Ephraim lounged in his chair, his hands in his pockets. "Really? That worries me. I wonder how the CJW will react to a lawsuit for libel." He stood up. "Look, I've had enough of you. Write what you want, but if there's any sexual innuendo in the story, your paper will hear from us."

He found Rebecca sitting in the lobby. "We're done," Ephraim said. "Brian is finalizing his notes. Let's go to the canteen for a coffee."

"How many coffees have you had today? You shouldn't drink too many."

"It's my first one today."

She looked hard into his eyes. "What kind of world is this? Even rabbis lie."

He told Laura about his encounter with Brian Ruby as they drove to the bar.

"Ephraim, darling," Laura said, "Brian Ruby has a dirty little mind, but my rival is very beautiful and is well-endowed in the breast department. It might have been her that first attracted you to her school idea. I bet a lot of men would find her very persuasive."

Ephraim pulled over to the side of the road and stopped the car. "Laura Burton, I love you and only you. Your bosom is well enough endowed for me. Don't be bothered by thoughts of Rebecca and stop referring to her as your rival. It's her school and only her school that intrigues me." He twisted in his seat, reached out and grasped her hair on either side of her face, pulled her towards him and kissed her hard and long on the lips.

She fell back into her seat, breathless. "Your actions speak louder than your words, but next time release my seatbelt before you attack me in the car," she said, smiling broadly and massaging her shoulder and breast.

CHAPTER 6

The Rabbi Makes A Decision

Marsha returned the next day, late in the afternoon. She hardly spoke as Ephraim drove home.

"You must be tired," he said to her sympathetically. "These shows can wear you out. Don't worry about the store. Laura seemed ok with it."

Marsha nodded. "I know. I called her a couple of times. That was a fantastic sale she pulled off. Thanks for helping out."

As they rode up in the elevator, Marsha looked at Ephraim accusingly. "There's something you haven't told me."

Ephraim froze — how did she find out? He felt like a little boy again, caught doing something wrong by an omniscient parent, like the time he and Alex skipped school to go to a Batman movie and as they stood in the ticket line, his mother suddenly appeared, staring angrily down at him. Then, too, he wondered how she had found out.

But this was more serious. The previous night, Laura had agreed to begin Jewish studies and he planned to wait until she was well into the course, before informing his mother.

"Something I haven't told you?" he gulped.

"We'll talk about it later."

While she unpacked, Ephraim prepared supper, concentrating on the task, trying to suppress all thoughts of the storm to come.

"I can explain everything," he said, as they sat in the eating area off the kitchen, eating a supper of bagels and lox.

"There's nothing to explain," Marsha countered. "Esther Feldman called me in Atlanta — she was so upset, 'I need a shoulder to cry on' — and told me all about Alex and his opera singer. You must have known and you said nothing to me."

A tidal wave of sweaty relief washed over him. "Ma, how could I say anything before Alex told his own parents? He was supposed to tell them over a month ago but kept putting it off. I was beginning to wonder whether it was serious."

She dropped her knife and fork onto her plate. "Didn't you try to talk him out of it?"

"Not really, ma. I met his bride-to-be. Polly Macrae. A very nice woman. They seemed very much in love. Alex insisted she was the one. Why should religion stand in the way?"

Marsha stared at Ephraim, disbelief in her eyes. "Ephraim Zimmerman, you are a rabbi. How can you talk like that? Religion is important — it's not just about Alex and his bride. The Feldmans are very unhappy and apparently her family is up in arms as well. Surely, a marriage should make everyone happy, not just the couple. How could you not at least argue with him?"

Because, he thought, I'm in the same boat. I couldn't even argue myself out of loving a non-Jewish girl. Aloud, he said, "Ma, Alex is my best friend. We're like brothers. We hold nothing back from each other. When he talked about Polly, he wasn't asking my advice, he was expressing his joy and it was genuine and sincere. She also made it clear she loves him and was happy with him. Isn't that what's important? Alex is not religious and opera is Polly's religion. Accommodating their careers will be the real challenge in their life together."

The entry buzzer sounded interrupting their conversation. Ephraim went down to the lobby to rescue his uncle from the vestibule. Marsha frowned as Avram entered. "Avram, this is not a good time to visit," Marsha said. "Freml and I are having a serious talk."

Avram shrugged his shoulders and sat down at the table. His eyes lit up as he noticed the bagels and lox. "So you think I can't be serious. You think Avram is nothing but jokes."

"No one would ever accuse you of that, Uncle Avram," Ephraim said, laughing. "Why don't you have some supper with us?" He was relieved that Avram had arrived, worried about where the conversation with his mother would lead.

Marsha explained: "We were discussing Alex Feldman and his Polly who is not Jewish. The Feldmans are very upset."

Avram, in the midst of spreading cream cheese on a bagel, stopped abruptly and glared at Ephraim. "I knew that boy was no good. I said so. He is sent by the devil. He is the evil eye, the hex. Freml, now you know what your so-called friend is like. Stay away from him. And you too, Marsha. Never mind his Ferrari."

"He doesn't have a Ferrari," Marsha said. "He has a wife."

"Ma, what are you saying?"

"So much for your friend who holds nothing back from you. They married secretly a couple of weeks ago at Toronto City Hall. Esther thinks Polly's pregnant, that's why they married so quickly."

"What kind of life will that child have? Better it should not be born," Uncle Avram declared, securing a slice of lox for his bagel.

Marsha snapped at him in disgust, "Avram, how can you say that?"

"Very simple. How will they raise the child? As a Jew? As a goy? As anything? No, better such people don't have children."

There was a moment of silence as Avram bit hungrily into his bagel.

"Uncle Avram," Ephraim said, "there are many mixed couples in Canada and many children from such marriages. Somehow the parents work out how the children will be raised. Of course, I'd like Alex to bring up his children as Jews but it's his and Polly's business — nobody else's. Surely the Almighty will not blame the child, if He attaches blame at all."

Avram exploded in anger but was in the process of swallowing a piece of his bagel. Coughing, he gasped for breath. His face turned red as bits of bagel and lox launched from his mouth. Ephraim leaped up and began pummelling him on his back.

"He's ok now," Marsha observed dryly as Avram stopped coughing. "If you hit him one more time, you'll do what the bagel nearly did."

"You're completely mishuga," Avram shouted at Ephraim. "How can a rabbi talk like that? It's clear in the Torah — a Jew can't marry a gentile."

"Uncle Avram, you know what a ger tzedek is?" Avram nodded. "Well, then if Polly converts, and the conversion is recognized by a Beit Din, then it's as though she's Jewish and it's not intermarriage."

Avram sighed. "Freml, it's not going to happen. Alex will not push it. You're loyal to your friend but you're a rabbi. You have to choose."

What will I choose? Ephraim thought. To give up Laura? To give up something that seems to make life fulfilling? Happiness we both cherish? Only five days ago they declared their love for each other — five days brimming with excitement and wonder, eager to be with each other, to talk, to touch. Every time he saw her, he marvelled at his great fortune, that someone like Laura could love him. He wanted her for a lifetime.

"Well," Avram concluded, "with you a rabbi, Marsha won't have to worry about you going astray. How are you getting along with the Zifkin girl? Gertie says you're all she talks about when she comes for her piano lessons."

Ephraim had no desire to pursue the conversation and merely shrugged his shoulders. Marsha rescued him. "That's enough now. Let's finish our meal and talk about something else. I'm going to see Esther and Morris tomorrow and try to calm them down. Life goes on."

In their nightly cell phone conversation, Ephraim told Laura of Alex and Polly and the reaction to their marriage.

"I never realized that Alex is a friend of yours," Laura said. "I used to talk quite openly about you, how hot you are."

"Alex fed it back to me but I was already in love with you."

"But then it's true what Frank claimed when I dropped him. He says you Jews have a network that surrounds the world."

"We're also trying to take over the world, one gentile woman at a time. Alex is ahead of me but I'll catch up."

He could hear her giggling. "How exciting! To think I'm part of a world conspiracy. Oh well, if I'm going to be captured and oppressed, at least it's with someone I like."

"Like? Just like?"

"Love, love, love. Ephraim, you're all I think about all day. How I long to be near you, to kiss you, to hold you."

"I think about you too. Today as I was driving out to the airport to pick up my mother, I daydreamed about you, how we were alone and I slowly undressed you and kissed you all over."

"And then what?"

"Then there was a loud horn behind me and all I could see in the rear-view mirror was the grill of a huge truck. I got out of there pretty quickly."

"Humph! A real lover would have ignored the truck and finished the daydream. But tell me, does your religion allow pre-marital sex? I'll go nuts if I have to wait until after my Jewish course."

He turned in his bed, pausing to think through the answer. "Good question. I haven't found an express prohibition but the laws stipulate I can't be alone with you unless you're my wife or my mother or a daughter."

He heard her giggling again. "Well, that makes it very simple. We'll invite our mothers to watch."

They bantered back and forth for a few minutes longer. Then she insisted that he read the Night Prayer to her. "My Jewish course starts on Monday and I want to feel into it."

The golden haze filled the room. He didn't want to face Elijah and pretended to sleep.

"Awake, my boy. It is useless to hide."

Ephraim sat up, still fearful, eyes cast down. "Hide? Hide from what?"

"Hide from your sinful ways."

The prophet was sitting on Ephraim's desk, a thin arm stretched out from the voluminous robe, pointing an accusing finger at him, the prophet's eyes dark and wide, glaring, angry.

"Your soul is rotting and because of this, the soul of your friend will rot as well. He has not wed one of our people. You knew and made no attempt to stop him. He who sees an Israelite about to commit a crime and does not try to reason with him and to dissuade him is just as guilty."

Ephraim reached out an imploring hand. "But Eliyahu, where it is clear that persuasion will have no effect, the duty to interfere is lifted."

The prophet stood up and glowered down at Ephraim. "Nonsense! You did not try to dissuade him because you too have been engulfed by carnal desire for a stranger in our midst. You who are a teacher, a leader, a learned man — yet you are prepared to wallow in the filth of this evil and to stand aside as others fall into the same pit. 'Hear, O Israel the Lord is our God, the Lord is One.' You say this many times during the day. Yet you and your friend align yourselves with women who will bring other gods into your house. Slowly you and others like you erode the power of Israel, desecrate the Covenant with the Almighty and will bring down His wrath upon us all."

"Eliyahu, there are many Israelites now and my friend and I are but two. Surely we cannot harm the power of Israel."

Elijah's anger and contempt were palpable. He impatiently walked up and down the bedroom. "Even the simple drip of a small drop of water digs a hole in the strongest rock. Consider the Cedars of Lebanon, that noble and powerful efflorescence of the Almighty. How did the hewers subdue this magnificent tree with their puny axes? Each of their feeble strokes removed a sliver, a chip, until the tree weakened and fell. Thus, you, and others like you, will slowly hew the tree of Israel."

Ephraim struggled to the side of the bed and resolutely faced the prophet. "Eliyahu, I hear you, but I find it difficult to accept that my behaviour will have such impact."

The prophet glared at him. "My son, hear my words and hear me carefully. What is a prophet? Our task is not merely to chronicle and to rave against the iniquities of Israel, to warn of impending doom. Recall the day the Almighty bested the priests of Baal. All morning the priests pleaded to their false god to accept their sacrifice. All morning their appeals were in vain and their sacrifice remained on their altar, untouched. Then it was the turn of Israel. I appealed to the Almighty to accept our sacrifice. It began to rain but I despaired not. The rain fell harder and the clouds grew thicker until day became like dusk. Suddenly, an enormous clap of thunder and a sheet of fire descended from the heavens and consumed our sacrifice. The Lord had answered my prayers. I remind you of this so that you will understand that it is not I that speaks to you but the spirit of the Almighty. Take heed."

Ephraim hung his head. "Eliyahu," he implored, "I love her."

The prophet seated himself on the desk. He spoke softly: "Do you believe, my son, that I have never felt the pangs of love and carnal desire? When the Lord instructed me to flee from Ahab, He sent me to the town of Zarephath in Sidon, there to be cared for by a widow. I sojourned three years with the widow. In the intimacy of her small hut, I was witness to her beauty of face and body. I could tell from her manner that she would have greeted my body with pleasure and shared her bed. I was mightily tempted but I reminded myself that I was there to serve the Almighty and that the woman was not of our people. I strove against the temptation many times during my stay with the widow and remained chaste throughout. You, too, are a servant of The One and must recognize your duty."

Elijah disappeared as the bedroom door opened and the ceiling light snapped on.

An alarmed Marsha stood in the doorway. "Freml, I heard you cry out. Are you alright?"

EPHRAIM

Ephraim had risen from his bed and was holding out a supplicating hand toward the departed Elijah. Squinting in the sudden light, he stared at his mother. "I must have been having a bad dream."

Marsha gently pushed him back into bed and tidied the covers. "Freml, I'm worried about you. You're walking and talking in your sleep, and I know there's something bothering you. Are your doubts bothering you?"

Ephraim closed his eyes. He wanted desperately to sleep. The argument with Elijah had drained him, left him exhausted and despairing. Only sleep could block out and put aside for a time the dilemma of his love for a Gentile woman and the obligations of his service to God. He sensed the ceiling light close and he drifted off.

He left early the next morning to catch the train to Guernsey. Haggard and drawn, he dozed the entire way. Once in Guernsey, he felt better. His ministry was succeeding as more people now showed up at the Saturday morning service and at the Sunday Breakfast Club. After lunch with the Petrovs on Saturday, he held the traditional bible studies class. Here, too, the level of interest had increased as more people attended and the question and answer period was spirited and stimulating.

The white-goateed man who had spoken at Rebecca's presentation leaned forward in his chair. "Rabbi, my name is Leo Abner and I'm a chemical engineer. I — "

"Watch out, Rabbi," Joe Petrov interrupted. "He's not just a chemical engineer. He's a PhD and a top research scientist in his specialty."

Leo Abner stood up and bowed and said good naturedly, "Thank you, Joe, for your kind introduction. Rabbi, what Joe really meant to say is I ask questions he has trouble answering." There was a ripple of appreciative laughter.

"As a rational scientist, imbued with the scientific method," Leo Abner continued, "I confess I'm sceptical whether a God exists. A famous astrophysicist, Carl Sagan, held the view that belief without evidence is superstition. If I follow this view to its logical conclusion, then I find myself questioning the evidence for the hypothesis that God exists and therefore the evidence for the Torah —or, for that matter, all the scriptures of all the religions — being the word of God also becomes suspect. If the Torah is not the word of God, then the foundation for the body of religious beliefs, rituals and traditions we call Judaism is completely undermined. Why should I, or for that matter any Jew, waste time studying and adopting a culture that persists in believing that a personal God exists and must be propitiated?"

Leo Abner sat down. There were grunts of approval and disapproval from other members of the audience. This was the ultimate question, thought Ephraim. Did it not frame his own doubts? He began to muster an answer, when Leo Abner stood up again.

"Rabbi, I'm particularly interested in this question because, as I said to the young lady who described her school idea earlier this summer, I would seriously encourage my son to send his two little girls there. My son intermarried and the children are being brought up as neither Jewish nor Christian. I told my son it's like feeding them warm diet pop — it will satisfy some of their thirst but lacks nutrition. So, despite everything I said, I believe the children should have a cultural identity and it seems to me our history and traditions would fit the bill. I'd like to hear your views."

Ephraim felt a sense of relief. "Well, Dr. Abner, you've partially answered your question. In spite of all your doubts, you see value in a Jewish education. The very fact that you're here today in the synagogue tells me you do feel the tug of Judaism. Personally, I have no trouble supporting a culture that has sustained our people for millennia through all the dark days of the Roman occupation of Israel, the pogroms and persecutions of the Christian era, and the holocaust. Like you, I see value in providing your grandchildren with a strong sense of identity.

"As for your other questions — does God exist? And even if He does exist, is the Torah the word of God? I agree with you that there seems to be no acceptable scientific evidence. To answer these questions, I rely on my faith. This may not satisfy you but I can think of no other answer. But even in science, there are many unexplained mysteries. What is this universe? Why is it here? What caused the Big Bang? What was before the Big Bang? How come all the laws of nature are exactly right for the development of an Earth and intelligent beings? I know that science has come up with ideas concerning these questions but these ideas are as speculative as my faith. In fact, in these mysteries I see evidence of a divine spirit which I call God."

Leo Abner nodded. "Rabbi, you're quite right. I believe it is fruitless to argue these points. I like to think that I'm a thoroughly secular man but when my son came home with the woman he wanted to marry — who by the way is a very fine woman and an excellent daughter-in-law — I was torn. It's a problem others of us here have experienced. Your family is lucky — they'll never have to face the same dilemma."

Ephraim should have let it go, but he couldn't. "If it makes you feel any better, I take a somewhat different view from the usual. As long as we lived in ghettos and our marriages were arranged, there was little danger of children straying across the line and intermarrying. When they did, there was indeed a huge stigma attached and the Jewish parents would begin Shiva. The offending child was ostracized, kicked out of the community. Remember the reaction of Tevya in *Fiddler on the Roof* when his daughter secretly marries the Catholic boy. In our time now, love between two people is recognized as a very powerful force. I find it difficult even as a rabbi to automatically condemn a love where one partner is not Jewish. Rather, I would try to persuade the non-Jewish partner to convert or at least to bring up the children as Jews. As for me personally, I'm as human as anyone."

There were a few more questions and then the session broke up. He was free for a couple of hours until the services marking the end of the Sabbath. He walked slowly through the downtown towards the park along the river, deep in thought. Yes, he was as human as anyone but what did that mean? Did he really have the right to jeopardize his calling? Would even these people in the Guernsey congregation, as secular as they might be, simply accept his love decision or would they shake their heads and roll their eyes? Would he continue to have their respect? Weren't they looking to him to set a standard of behaviour? His duty said to him that he should break off with Laura before their relationship went even further. It would be hard for both of them, because they truly loved each other. But perhaps a little pain now was better than the prolonged crisis he envisioned if they should announce their plans to marry.

He reached the river and sauntered along the embankment. It was a mild summer day, a refreshing breeze blowing in from the lake. He stopped to watch an enormous ore laker slide gracefully by on its downriver journey, its wake bubbling the waters behind it and spreading out to the shores on either side. He sat down on a bench overlooking the water, removed his hat and suit coat and loosened his tie. The serenity of the scene did not still the turmoil in his mind.

Life would be far easier for him if he had simply fallen in love with Rebecca. Everyone would marvel at the match. It would be seen as absolutely right, for him, for her, and of course, he smiled wryly, for Uncle Avram. If he persisted in his love of Laura, even if she converted, the family would be very disappointed. His mother would eventually come around, of that he felt certain, and he didn't particularly care about Uncle Avram's feelings. The real question was could he continue his career? Would the Jewish community accept an intermarried rabbi? Of this, he was not certain but had grave doubts. Therefore his career was in jeopardy. But what was stronger — his career or his love? A king of England had given up his throne for love. But being a rabbi was not just a career like Alex had a career. A rabbi was a calling, a vocation, service to a higher order and to the community. Yes, he loved Laura, deeply, profoundly. But should he sacrifice his calling for a personal obsession? They would both be hurt by the break-up. He remembered the two nights when he thought their romance was over and how bereaved he had felt. She would be terribly upset as well but in the end it would be better for her. Would she have been able to learn and accept the myriad, detailed Jewish rules and regulations required for life with a rabbi? Or would she come to resent the whole thing? And if she could not make the adjustments and he had to give up his career, would he come to resent their love?

He watched the blue river water gliding past. There was so much certainty to the journey of this river. It would flow past Detroit, through Lake Erie and then fling itself over Niagara Falls, speed along on the Niagara River and flow placidly through Lake Ontario and into the St. Lawrence to the ocean. But the droplets of water that made up the river had no such certainty. Some could be pulled off to the cities, some might be sucked into the Welland Canal, or find themselves in eddies of backwater stuck in a bay or trapped in a patio pool, or meet the tidal swell that came up the St. Lawrence from the Atlantic and get pushed back, or get drawn up into the air to grow a cloud and sail over the world.

The westering sun beat down on him. He lolled, stretched out on the bench, his suit coat pillowing his head.

He heard his name called and saw a familiar figure walking purposefully along the path towards him.

"Foolish boy," Elijah said as he came up to him. "You are not like a drop of water which has no life but goes where the whim of the Almighty sends it. You are of Israel and possess the will to do good or evil, to pick one course or the other, to obey the Almighty's commandments or to ignore them. I remind you — whenever our people put aside the worship of the One and followed other gods, disaster overtook them. Our Lord brooks not idolatry, heresy, faithlessness, sin. Be mindful of my words."

Ephraim sat up and leaned forward. He wanted to tell Elijah that he had thought it over and would break with the Gentile woman. He opened his eyes but Elijah was gone.

Normally on these weekends he rented a car. This time he had opted to go by train and since there were only early morning and evening departures, he spent most of Sunday with the Petrovs at the beach in front of their house. They drove him to the station for the seven pm departure.

He watched the flat farmlands covered with hay and corn stretching out on either side of the speeding train. The car wasn't crowded and he had a double seat to himself. He mulled over his decision to break off with Laura, rehearsing ways in which he might handle it. The train stopped in London and there was a brief bustle of movement as passengers got on and off. Then the train eased out of the station. He went back to his musings.

"Is this seat taken?" asked a soft sultry voice.

He looked up and knew in that instant that his decision had collapsed.

She sat down beside him. He was so startled that all he could do was reach out and hold her hands.

"You told me which train you were taking. I took an earlier train to London. I wanted to talk to you and I didn't want to wait until you finally got home." There were tears in her eyes. "I came to tell you it was all over between us. I didn't feel it would work, I told my mother what I was up to and she was very relieved. But when I see you now, I can't do it. I just love you too much."

He pulled her close and kissed away the tears. "Sweetheart, I was going to tell you the same thing — that we should break it off. I thought a lot about it and I didn't see how we could succeed. But as soon as you appeared, I knew I couldn't do it. No, for better or worse, we're stuck with each other. I can't believe that loving you is a sin. I'll give up everything for you."

"No, you won't. I'll learn what I have to. We both believe in the same God. So it's just a matter for me to learn some other traditions. I can become as good a rebbetsyn as anyone."

He held her off from him. "Where did you learn that word?"

She pulled herself back into his arms. "From that encyclopaedia of all knowledge — Google."

He buried his face in her hair and squeezed her tightly against him.

"Go easy," she gasped. "Even a rebbetsyn has to breathe. You know, my mother, who is very wise, suggested I write to you, that if I met with you, I wouldn't be able to say goodbye. But I couldn't write you a Dear John letter. What would I say? 'Dear Ephraim, I don't believe I have the courage and the strength to love you.' No, I felt I owed it to you to tell you this personally. The truth is I don't have the courage or the strength not to love you."

They were interrupted by the train conductor collecting tickets. Ephraim waited until the conductor had moved a few rows away. "I adore you," he said. "I want to marry you."

"You still haven't courted me properly. So far, it's been a couple of bar nights."

"You haven't counted this train ride," he said, grinning.

She reached up and grabbed him by the ears. "I've paid for my ticket and yours is covered by expenses. The train ride doesn't count."

They leaned into each other, giggling like two schoolchildren. For the rest of the trip, they talked about how they would proceed with Laura's path to conversion and when Ephraim's family would be informed.

CHAPTER 7

The Rabbi Lays Out A Strategy

July drifted into August. Ephraim had sought out the help of a fellow graduate who acted as Laura's mentor. The evening course she was taking was specifically designed for those seeking conversion. Ephraim anxiously gauged her reaction as the weeks slipped by, offering advice and explaining some of the more abstruse rules.

"You don't have to know everything," he urged her on one occasion. "You just have to learn how to keep a kosher home."

"Nonsense," she said. "I have to learn how to behave in the synagogue, what to do and what not to do on the Sabbath and holidays, and everything else I need to know so as not to embarrass you. I'm going to be a rebbetsyn you can be proud of. I even have to change some of my vocabulary. My mentor reminded me very sternly the other day that if I get excited, I have to say something other than 'sweet Jesus.'"

"You've never said that in my presence."

"There you are. The training is working."

They confined their dates to the weekday evenings after nine. They spent a lot of time in the bar on Eglinton Avenue, where they could sit close together in the dimly lit obscurity. Alex and Polly joined them occasionally and one evening invited Ephraim and Laura to their new condo apartment on King Street West.

The building boasted an Olympic sized swimming pool on the ground floor adjacent to the lobby. Large glass doors down one side of the pool were opened wide to let in the warm, summer air. Ephraim was aware of the looks of admiration he received from the other women as he stood outside the women's change room waiting for Laura. When she appeared in a form hugging one piecer, he felt an immediate rush of desire. They splashed into the water together, playfully chasing each other up and down the pool, catching hold of each other, hands on legs and thighs and breasts. They tread water at the deep end, arms around each other, then kissed and slowly sank beneath the surface. They broke apart and came up for air.

"Ephraim," she whispered into his ear, "I don't think I can wait six months. I'm starting to feel like a nun."

"I can't wait either," he whispered back. "We'll work something out."

Alex came to their rescue. "When you finish your swim, bring your clothes up. You can change in our guest room."

The guest room was only slightly smaller than the master bedroom and connected to a full bathroom.

"Since you're not married yet, I'll have to act as chaperone," Alex insisted, a mischievous smile lighting up his face. Polly grabbed him by an ear and marched him out.

Ephraim closed the door to the guest room. He and Laura stood facing each other. Ephraim slid the straps of her swimsuit off her shoulders and pulled the suit down gently, kissing her body as he went. He lingered on her breasts. She pulled down his swimsuit, made even tighter by a full erection, and fondled his genitals. It so maddened him that he grasped her tightly, dragged her down to the carpeted floor and entered her. Even after the orgasmic burst, he continued to thrust until they lay exhausted. Ephraim rolled over on to his back and Laura crawled on top of him, chucking her head under his chin. Absentmindedly, he ran his hands down her back and up the incline of her buttocks. He felt supremely happy.

"That was fabulous," she murmured. "I've been itching for weeks for this. Of course, now you've had your fill, my attraction is gone."

He slapped her playfully on the buttocks. "That's your punishment for saying bad things. Now I'm completely enslaved by you. All you've done is whet my appetite."

They showered together, soaping each other. They dressed and joined Polly and Alex in the dining room for coffee and cakes.

Polly assured Ephraim, "Alex bought the cakes at the Clarke Street Solly's so everything is kosher."

"Except our women," Alex said. "They're not kosher."

Laura wagged a finger at him. "Mind what you say. Soon I will be." She told them about her Jewish studies course and how fast she was learning. "My rabbi mentor says I'll be able to convert in maybe five months. Then Ephraim and I can marry and live happily ever after."

"Good for you, Laura," Polly said. "Alex and I also had conversion problems. I've had to convert him to a taste for opera and he's making good progress. These bankers think the world of finance is everything, so it's been an uphill battle."

Alex laughed. "Yes, I've even used quantitative analysis to come up with important insights into opera — nine out of ten sopranos die by the end of the opera."

Ephraim shook his head. "Polly, you better work some more on him."

Alex carefully poured coffee into their cups and pushed the tray of pastries toward Laura and Ephraim. "When do you plan to tell your families?" he asked.

"My mother's asked to meet Ephraim and that'll be a couple of nights from now," Laura said as she helped herself to a pastry.

"How are your parents taking it?" Ephraim asked.

There was a moment of silence.

"My family's reaction is mixed," Polly said between swallows of coffee and cake. "My father thought I'd end up marrying another opera singer, and he'd never see me again. Once he got over the fact that I'd married a Jew and discovered that Alex was an investment banker, he seemed to accept the whole thing. My mother is having a more difficult time. She always wanted me to marry a Scot to keep the family heritage and tradition alive. So she hasn't quite come around yet. And Alex didn't help when he suggested we call our kids the MacFeldmans."

Ephraim gazed affectionately at his friend. "I thought investment bankers had to exercise great sensitivity in their deal making."

"Yeah, I should have been more thoughtful, and saved my glib for you. Dammit, Freml, Polly and I are not kids. We're mature adults capable of taking responsible decisions. We can't be held to everybody's dream idea of what constitutes the right marriage. My own parents had a very rough start with our marriage. I did it all the wrong way. We decided to present a fait accompli by marrying first. I thought my mother was going to have a breakdown when

I came with the news. My father just sat there with his mouth open. He's a criminal lawyer — you'd think nothing would surprise or shock him."

Ephraim nodded. "I know about your mother. She was so upset, she called my mother in Atlanta. Then I got an earful because I didn't try to talk you out of it."

Alex laughed. "She didn't realize you were wrestling with the same problem."

"Problem?" Polly snapped and jumped out of her chair to tower over Alex.

Alex reached out an arm, encircled her waist and pulled her onto his lap. "Wrong choice of a word, my sweet. In business lingo, I would've said 'challenge' or 'opportunity.' That's it. Ephraim is wrestling with the great opportunity to integrate Judaism and Catholicism."

Laura looked lovingly at Ephraim. "Hardly integration. I have to convert."

"There's something wrong with a world where ethnic and religious loyalties are more important than love," Alex complained. "Why should Laura have to convert? OK, she has to learn something about Jewish law and custom to keep our rabbi friend here happy. But why should our parents or the community care? Wouldn't it be nice if everyone simply said — 'oh, what a lovely couple — they seem so happy together — let's have a party.'"

"I think it's the party you're after," Ephraim said. "How are your parents now with the marriage?"

"Thanks to Polly, they're coming around — sort of. We had a get together at my parents' apartment with Polly and her parents. At first everyone was stiff and formal — you could cut the tension in the air. Mr. Macrae talked about his family heritage that went back centuries and was documented in churches and grave sites. Freml, you know the history of most of us. My great grandparents arrived in 1901 with fifty cents between them, along with a change of name because some bureaucrat couldn't handle the real name. No documents, no family history. It confirmed his view that Polly was marrying well below her class."

Polly, still sitting on Alex's lap, kissed him on the forehead. "I'm the apple of my father's eye. He would have been upset even if you were the King of Scotland."

Alex hugged her. "Anyway, Polly is first and foremost an entertainer. She sat down at my mother's piano and played and sang that old Jewish wedding staple Bluebird of Happiness and followed it up with Auld Lang Syne. By the time she finished, everyone was in tears, including me, and we all hugged and kissed. Then my father got out his best single malt and the formality was gone. So that got us past the introduction."

Polly continued, "Our fathers seem to be ok and try to be welcoming with both of us. But our mothers still seem upset. They accept us like they've no choice."

"Freml, get togethers can be pretty tense at times. You know me, Freml, in company I like to relax and kibitz. My M&A meetings are more relaxed than when we have dinner with our parents."

Polly kissed him again on the forehead. "Don't worry, Alex. They'll come around. We're such a fine example, how can anyone not love us?"

Two nights later, Laura and Ephraim had their own first taste of a recalcitrant parent. Laura opened the door and looked approvingly at Ephraim in his summer slacks and open shirt. They embraced and kissed. Laura led him into the living room where Mrs. Burton sat on a sofa, a newspaper in her lap.

"Mommy, this is Ephraim Zimmerman."

Mrs. Burton did not get up but held up a hand which Ephraim grasped. She quickly withdrew her hand.

"Mrs. Burton, I'm happy to meet you. Laura is always high in her praise of her mother."

There was an awkward silence. Ephraim and Laura stood like wax figures while Mrs. Burton stared past them.

Finally, she looked directly at Ephraim. "To be honest, Mr. Zimmerman, I am not happy to meet you. I believe my daughter is making a terrible mistake. I've nothing against you or your religion, but it's not her religion or heritage. I know you'll both insist that you love each other, and I'm sure you do, but love is blind. It's up to us on the sidelines to exercise judgement."

For a long moment, Ephraim was seized by an irresistible sense of sadness. An image pushed itself into his mind — an image of a verdant Earth suddenly smashed by a huge meteor. He stared deep into Mrs. Burton's eyes and noted the look of unflinching hostility on her face. She was an older version of Laura, a little portly in her late fifty's, with the same pouting lips and straight brown hair falling to her shoulders. Like Laura, she spoke her mind.

Laura sat down beside her mother and held her hands. "Please, mommy, be nice to him. He means so much to me." Tears flowed down the cheeks of both women.

Ephraim knelt in front of them and put his hands on theirs. "Mrs. Burton, I love your daughter very much and we both want you to be part of our lives. We —"

"How can I be part of your lives?" she interrupted. "You can't even eat in my house. Christmas is important to our family. You won't be able to join us and neither will Laura when she becomes Jewish. And if you have children, what then? How can I enjoy them? They won't be able to come here. I'll be an outsider in your lives."

"Mrs. Burton, do you think we can't visit you because of our kosher laws?" She nodded.

"You must have family or friends that have diet restrictions?"

She looked at him suspiciously. "Yes, my sister's a vegetarian, one friend is diabetic, and another must eat low fat foods. So what?"

"Do they eat here and do you adjust for their diets."

She nodded. "You're about to tell me that your laws are just another diet."

"In essence, they are — just like a special diet. Once you know what we're allowed, it'll be very simple to accommodate us. As for Christmas, I see no reason why we can't be part of the festivities. If you make the traditional Christmas dinner, I won't be able to eat it and I can't sing the carols but I can still celebrate with you. Laura and I have talked about Jesus and Christmas and I won't stand in her way. And you'll be every bit a grandmother to our children as my mother."

Mrs. Burton shook her head sadly. "I wish I could believe all that. I know you're sincere but I can't see it happening. You are Jewish, Laura will become Jewish, and your children will be Jewish. You'll all feel more at home on the Jewish side of the family."

Still kneeling before the two women, Ephraim took Mrs. Burton's hands in his. "I make you a solemn promise, Mrs. Burton. I will do everything I can to make you feel part of our lives."

She still shook her head but the hostility was draining from her face and she did not withdraw her hands. "How can I accept your promise? We've been taught for years to hate the Jews because they killed Christ. Yes, I know the Pope has apologized for the centuries of persecution but he never said you were innocent. And now, I'm supposed to welcome you to my life as my son-in-law. Not only you but my own daughter and eventual grandchildren. I'm not intolerant — I'm happy that Laura is employed by your mother who treats her with kindness and respect. But I still find this all too difficult."

"I understand," Ephraim said and lifted her hands to his lips. "Please don't think that I'm being smart or glib when I say that I and every Jew living today had nothing to do with the death of Christ. Mathew put a curse on us but it is up to God, not Man, to judge us. We don't accept the divinity of Christ and if that's a sin, again it is up to God to judge, nobody else. Therefore, you should have no qualms of conscience. One more thing. At the time of his existence, Jesus was very much a Jew. He would have followed the same kosher laws that I follow today. He, too, was a rabbi, and he would have studied the same basic texts that I studied. I'm hoping this will make it easier for you to accept me."

He spoke sincerely, placatingly and was rewarded with the semblance of a smile on Mrs. Burton's face.

"I suppose I should be flattered that there's a rabbi kneeling in front of me. Laura tells me that Jews never bow or kneel.

Ephraim smiled. "Goddesses are an exception."

Mrs. Burton laughed heartily. "Watch out, Laura, he has a silver tongue." Still beaming, she went on: "You're a likable fellow, Rabbi Zimmerman, but all I can think of is you're stealing my daughter away."

Laura reached up and fondled her mother's chin. "Oh, mommy, you're selling me short. I wasn't exactly a piece of merchandise waiting to be shoplifted. I fell in love with him the moment he walked into the store that first night just as we were closing. I pretended to concentrate on my count until I got control of myself."

Laura left the sofa and pulled Ephraim up. "Look at him, mommy. Isn't he beautiful? He's also very wise and educated and tries to please me. Like all men, he sometimes says dumb things but then apologizes. Mommy, I've never been so happy."

Ephraim blushed as both women looked him up and down like a prize horse. Mrs. Burton stood up and embraced Laura. "Don't worry, sweetie, I'll always be your mother, no matter what."Looking at Ephraim, she said. "You better be nice to her or you'll hear from me. Now, let's have a cup of coffee."

I don't believe my mother loves me any less, thought Ephraim as he drove home later that night, but I don't think she'll come around as quickly as Mrs.

Burton did. True, Mrs. Burton wasn't in total agreement, more like grudging acceptance for the sake of her daughter. Nevertheless, the atmosphere at the coffee table was relaxed and occasionally genial.

When to tell his mother? He had explained to Mrs. Burton that Laura should get further on in her Jewish studies before involving his mother. Then she would better understand that he and Laura were serious and that he might be able to salvage his career as a rabbi.

"Your mother sounds tougher than I am," Mrs Burton said. "Or was I selected as the guinea pig to test the waters?"

"No, mommy," Laura answered. "I insisted that Ephraim meet you today. I can't bear to keep secrets from you and you knew how I felt about him. Mommy, I know you're unhappy about my leaving our religion, but Ephraim isn't asking me to. He made it clear it was my decision — that he'd give up his vocation and do something else if necessary. No, mommy, it's my decision. His religion is much more a part of him and I want to be a real supportive partner."

"No wonder you love her, Rabbi Zimmerman," Mrs. Burton said, fondly stroking Laura's cheek. "She's breaking all the feminist rules for you."

He loved her all the more then, and toyed with the idea of telling his mother immediately. However, in a month, he would be leaving for Nova Scotia and would be away September and October. In November, he would return for a brief holiday and Laura would be close to finishing her studies. That would be the time.

But over the next few days, his carefully thought out strategy began to unravel.

CHAPTER 8

The Enemy Strikes

"Freml, come to the store right away. Something terrible's happened."

Ephraim was writing his sermon for the weekend when his cell phone rang. His mother's voice, anxious and fearful, was loud enough that Nitsky looked up from his work. It was a few minutes before ten so Marsha must have just reached the store.

"What is it, ma? Are you ok? Is anyone hurt?"

"Just come. I've called the police and mall security is here." She hung up.

Sholom Nitsky grabbed him as he made to leave the office. "I'll drive you there."

A yellow police tape was already up around the store when they arrived, panting. Two police officers and a mall security agent were directing early shoppers away. Marsha came out of the store and pulled Ephraim to the store window. Coal black graffiti plastered the glass with its message of hate: a swastika took up the left hand side of the window followed by the words 'jew suks' and below them: '1- r mony 2 – r womn.'

Marsha was beside herself with fear and indignation. "You're supposed to protect us," she shrieked at the mall security supervisor as he joined the group. "How does this happen inside the mall?"

The supervisor was a heavy set man with a florid face which flared even redder as he faced Marsha's accusations. "Madam, we will get to the bottom of this, I can assure you. We'll examine the surveillance tapes and see if we can spot the perpetrators. Nothing like this has ever happened in our mall before."

Sholom Nitsky pursed his lips and shook his head. "This is awful, Ephraim. I thought we had seen the last of this a long time ago."

Marsha began to cry and buried her face in Ephraim's shoulder. He held her close solicitously.

"Madam," said one of the policemen, his notebook flipped open and pencil poised. "I'm looking at the message. Have you had any difficult dealings with any customer recently?"

Marsha raised her face and looked squarely into the policeman's eyes. "I never have difficulties with my customers. This was not done by a customer."

The policeman pushed on. "The second part of the message, I believe, is about women. Have there been any problems with your staff?"

Marsha shook her head. "Not that I'm aware. There are only three employees — one full timer who will be here at one o'clock and two part timers who work mostly on weekends and busy times."

"Well," said the policeman, "I don't think whoever did it has English as a first language unless the misspellings were deliberate. Why don't we step into the store so I can get all the information I need, including the phone numbers of your staff."

Marsha had calmed down, and Ephraim did not follow her into the store. A couple of photographers had shown up and were busy taking pictures of the store window. Ephraim recognized one of them — Brian Ruby from the CJW.

"Hey, Rabbi," Ruby called out as he stepped back against the yellow tape to snap the whole window, "come to view the latest affront to our people?"

"My mother owns the store," Ephraim replied.

Ruby looked at him with interest, shouldered his camera, and came over to the two rabbis with his notepad and pencil out. "What do you know about this? Does your mother have any enemies? Or was this just random? You know, pick a Jewish store window, any Jewish store window. Whoever did it knew your mother is Jewish."

Ephraim didn't answer. A gnawing suspicion had begun to percolate through him and raised troubling feelings of guilt. He broke the awkward silence by introducing Ruby to Sholom Nitsky.

"This is very bad," Nitsky said. "I hope your paper will hit this hard and warn your readers to be vigilant."

Ruby shrugged. "Sure, I'll lay it on thick but how are we supposed to be vigilant? Stay all night in our store in a closed, so-called secure mall in case some anti-Semitic asshole comes sneaking along. Maybe it's the authorities who should be vigilant. You'll see, I'll write this up as another example of neo-Nazi activity but the police will downplay it as a random malicious prank. But I think there's something more here. The money part of the message is standard tripe but the second part about women tells me sex has reared its ugly head. This could be a warning to somebody."

Sholom shook his head. "I think your speculation is far fetched. This is not the only example of hateful graffiti in this neighbourhood. There's a gang of anti-Semites alive and well and the sooner they're identified and dealt with, the better off we'll all be."

"Amen," said Ephraim.

Sholom returned to the Institute but Ephraim stayed behind until the yellow police tape was removed and the window was cleaned of its offensive message. Customers entering the store loudly proclaimed their support for Marsha and condemned the state of young people today. It was strange, Ephraim thought, that everyone assumed vandalizing with graffiti was something only irresponsible teenagers do.

When he saw that Marsha was fully occupied, he wandered into the food court and called Laura.

"Do you think it's Frank?" she asked after he described what had happened and the nature of the message.

"That's my feeling. We'll know more if the surveillance tapes show us anything. We're meeting with mall security tomorrow morning to review the tapes. But if it's Frank, how did he learn about us?"

She sighed into the cell phone. "My sweet innocent rabbi. We haven't exactly hidden our feelings for each other. We meet in the mall food court and other public places. All he needed was to see us together a couple of times and he'd know. He's completely racist. It must totally gall him that he lost his girl to a Jew and a rabbi at that. Your mother doesn't deserve this. I feel terrible like I've brought it on."

"Sweetheart," Ephraim said emphatically, "put that thought out of your mind. We're the victims, not the guilty if indeed it is Frank. Let's wait until tomorrow to see what evidence there is. Security said they'll stay close to the store over the next few days, so you don't have to worry. But if he shows up and bothers you, just call the police."

Ephraim and Marsha met with Richard Turner, mall security head, in his office the next morning at 9:30. To Ephraim's surprise, Laura was also there along with a plainclothes police officer who was introduced as Detective Dave Wilson.

"Hope you don't mind, Mrs. Zimmerman," Dave Wilson said. "I thought it'd be useful if your assistant was here as well, since, I understand, she's in the store almost as much as you."

"I don't mind at all," Marsha said as she and Laura embraced. Ephraim tried to look nonchalant as he nodded to Laura.

Mounted on a side table was a large television screen. A video player and a small pile of tapes sat in front of Turner.

"The way I figure it," Turner began, "the incident took place shortly after the mall closed at nine pm. We usually allow a half hour for stragglers to exit the mall before locking up. I think the party or parties came along, saw nobody around, and took advantage and vandalized the window. There is no direct surveillance of that space but we do have the tapes of all the people leaving the mall during that period. If I'm right, then the guilty would have been the last or close to the last to leave. These are the tapes from the doors closest to the store and run from 9:10 to 9:30."

They watched the tapes unfold on the screen. Most of the images were of the backs of people. Ephraim recognized one familiar figure as she resolutely walked out of the mall.

"That's me," said Laura. "I've closed and I'm on my way home."

"As you left the store, did you see anything that struck you as odd?" Wilson asked.

"No, just some ladies with shopping bags heading for their cars."

They watched a few more minutes of tape from various doors but nothing stood out.

"What are we supposed to look for?" Ephraim asked. "People behaving suspiciously?"

"Anybody you recognize," Turner said. "Maybe people you've seen hanging around the store."

"There are the Gillicuddys," Laura called out as a tall man and short woman appeared. "They were in just before closing to exchange a wall clock. Mrs. Zimmerman, that's the second clock that's malfunctioned. I really think we should talk to our supplier about their products."

"You're absolutely right, Laura. First thing when we open the store."

"Ladies," said Turner, "let's concentrate on the task at hand."

The tapes showed dwindling numbers of people as the time neared 9:30 pm. Seconds passed and on some of the tapes there was no one. Then Ephraim caught his breath and stifled a gasp. On the tape at the exit door nearest the store, a single tall, burly figure, head inclined as though he were looking for something on the floor could be seen walking slowly towards the exit. Turner stopped the tape.

"My guess is this is the culprit. He knows he's being taped so he's keeping his head down. He's not rushing — trying to look unconcerned. Unfortunately, it's probably impossible to make a positive identification."

"There is something vaguely familiar about that man. Perhaps I've seen him or somebody like him in the mall," said Marsha, frowning.

Turner ran the tape back and then played it again. Ephraim was conflicted. He was certain the man in the tape was Frank — not just because of the burly figure but also from the way he walked, a kind of waddle with the body swaying from side to side. To voice the identity might lead to more questions and reveal prematurely to his mother his plan to marry Laura. Yet if he said nothing, he could be exposing his mother to further outrage. On the other hand, Frank could simply deny he was the person on the tape, or even if he admitted it, he would deny the vandalism. Yet, if he were questioned by police, it might be enough to persuade him to leave them alone.

Wilson was looking at Laura. "Even if you're not certain, if you suspect who that might be, please tell us. Trust us to investigate properly. Nobody wants to get innocent people in trouble, least of all the police."

Ephraim sensed the conflict going on in Laura. She said nothing and stared down at the table.

Marsha's frown suddenly turned to enlightenment. "Laura, he looks like your boyfriend. He hasn't been to the store recently but I sometimes see him in the mall."

Laura looked at Ephraim uneasily. "It does look like my former boyfriend," she said hesitantly. "But we broke off months ago."

Wilson was busy taking notes. "Have you seen him since you broke off?" he asked.

Laura shook her head. "No, he's called me a few times but I told him no deal."

"What's his name and why did you break off?"

"His name is Frank Yanovich and I dropped him because…"

"Go on. Because…"

"Because he wanted me to quit my job. Because I'm working for a Jew. I'm sorry, Mrs. Zimmerman, I feel like I've brought all this on."

Marsha reached over a reassuring arm. "You've got nothing to be sorry for. You're smart to have dropped him. You're too nice a girl to get mixed up with people like that."

"Wait a minute," Turner said. "If this Frank did the dirty deed, is he blaming Mrs. Zimmerman for stealing away his girl? It doesn't make sense. Do you have another boyfriend?"

Laura reddened, her eyes turned sharply down. "Yes, but I cannot tell you. It's a secret for the time being."

"Dammit," Turner expostulated. "That secret might be the key to this whole thing. If your new boy friend is Jewish, that would explain an awful lot."

Laura swallowed hard. "He is," she said. "We have agreed to keep it secret for the time being. Frank may have seen us together."

"But, Laura," Marsha asked, "even if he saw you together, how would he know your new boyfriend is Jewish? Does Frank know him?"

"Who is it?" Turner asked.

"Hang on, Richard," Wilson said. "I think we've got enough to go on for the moment. We have a possible motive, but jealousy does not justify the crime. Frank Yanovich is not unknown to us. We'll have a little talk with him."

The meeting broke up and the policeman left. At Ephraim's request for a private space to discuss store security with his mother and her assistant, Turner directed them to a small conference room down the hall from his office.

Laura knew what was coming and sat down at the table, picking fluff off her skirt. Marsha looked at Ephraim quizzically. "What is it, Freml?" she said, her voice betraying uneasiness.

Ephraim closed the door. "Sit down, ma. There's something you should know."

Marsha saw the disconsolate look on Laura's face and the grim determination on Ephraim's. "Does this have something to do with Laura's secret?"

Ephraim nodded. "Yes, ma. I'm Laura's new boyfriend. We love each other. We plan to marry."

There was a long silence as Marsha stared first at Ephraim and then at Laura, bewilderment on her face. "Marry?"

Ephraim and Laura both nodded. "Yes, ma. We expect to marry either late this year or early next year."

Marsha said nothing but continued to look at them.

"There's no date set yet," Ephraim said. "We're waiting until Laura finishes her Jewish studies."

"But you're a rabbi!" Marsha shrieked. "A Jewish rabbi. How can you marry a shiksa?"

"Please, Mrs. Zimmerman," Laura stood up and walked around the table beside Marsha. "I'm going to convert. I'm already part way through my course and the rabbi teaching me says I'll be ready in November or December." She reached out and put a hand on Marsha's shoulder.

Marsha struck the arm away angrily. "Don't you dare touch me. I treated you like a daughter and you betrayed me. Sneaking around behind my back, trapping my son."

Both women burst into tears. Ephraim signalled to Laura to return to her seat. He moved over beside his mother. "Ma, please don't blame Laura. When we discovered our love, I was the one who insisted we keep it secret."

"You're a rabbi," Marsha sobbed. "You'll never be able to practise. You're ruining your career. Can you not break it off before it's too late?"

"We tried, ma. We can't. I love her too much."

Marsha stood up, leaned over the table, and glared at Laura. "And what about you? When he marries you, he's out of a job. If you really loved him, you'd leave him alone."

Ephraim cradled his arm around Marsha, and pulled her back to her chair. "Ma, listen to me. Laura will be confirmed Jewish before we marry. According to Jewish law, marriage to a converted Jew is not intermarriage. Yes, you're right. There may be synagogues or communities who will still reject us, but there may be others who will not."

Marsha shook her head. "I knew there was something going on with you. Rebecca called me one day and said she hadn't heard from you, were you ok? Then you'd go off to the Clarke Street shul for the evening service and not come home until midnight. But I never thought this. You told your uncle you weren't interested in marriage right now. You wanted to get into your work. What happened with that? You'll never get into your work now." She turned to Laura. "How do we know you're not marrying him for his money?"

"Money? What money?" Ephraim said. "Right now Laura earns about as much as I do. The Chevra Kadisha Institute doesn't pay a lot over and above expenses."

"Does Rabbi Nitsky know of your plans?"

"I haven't told him yet. I wanted to wait until Laura was confirmed. I've discussed the concept of a Jew marrying a converted Jew, and he seemed favourable to the idea but it was in the context of my officiating at a wedding. I don't know what his reaction will be when I tell him."

Marsha pressed her hands to her head. "What a sorry situation you've created, both of you. Freml, you can forget about your job with Rebecca. On religious and personal grounds, she's going to be awfully hurt. And what about your family, Laura? Are they happy with your choice of husband?"

"My mother is not happy. She's as loyal to her religion as you are to yours, Mrs. Zimmerman. Plus my decision to convert makes it even harder for her. Nevertheless, she's resigned to the idea and I think she likes Ephraim. Most of the rest of the family, my uncles, aunts, cousins, don't seem to care. Mrs. Zimmerman, when I finish my course and convert, I'll be a Jewish girl marrying a rabbi, and you'll have a Jewish daughter-in-law. I will be proud to be Ephraim's rebbetsyn and help him in his work."

Marsha stood up and paced up and down the small conference room. "This is complete madness. You're both insane. How can you learn in six months what takes other women years of education? Rebecca could be his rebbetsyn. She grew up in a religious family, went to Jewish parochial schools since kindergarten, and is an accredited teacher. She knows all the rules but more importantly has a feel for things Jewish. It's built into her from an early age — it's in her DNA. It's not like buying a new spring outfit."

Ephraim went over to Marsha, held her, and brought her back to the table. "Ma, it's unfair what you're saying. Of course, it'll take time for Laura to develop the right experience. But she's committed to do it. You can definitely help her. Ma, we love each other. Surely, love has to count for something."

Marsha grasped her head and swayed from side to side. "Excuse me, I can't think anymore. All I see is my son throwing away his life and career. I'm going along now to open the store. Laura, I don't want you anymore. I can't work alongside you and pretend nothing's happened. Pick up any personal stuff you have in the store and go. My accountant will send you whatever we owe plus severance."

EPHRAIM

"Ma," Ephraim objected, "please don't just fire her. Think about it. I'm going to marry her one of these days. Will you never accept us as husband and wife? Don't do things now that will make it difficult later on. You're upset now. But you know you like Laura. Can you not give it some time?"

"I like Laura as an employee, as an assistant in the store. Yes, she's very good and has brought in additional customers and business. But I never saw her as a wife for my son. The idea is frankly… revolting. It's not just intermarriage that's bothering me. If you were like Alex, I'd probably come to accept it like Esther and Morris. But you're a rabbi. You might as well have skipped your years at Yeshiva U. I'm starting to think they were right. You need help. Maybe I will accept Laura some day but right now I need some breathing space. She has to go."

"Ma, you're blaming her but I'm just as guilty. She didn't go after me. I don't feel entrapped. She's not wrecking my career — by converting, she's trying to save it."

Laura had been silent, head down, tears occasionally dripping onto her lap. Now she stood up and walked to the door. "Ephraim, there's no point in arguing further at the moment. If we do, we're bound to say something in anger that's hurtful and make it impossible to reconcile later. I'm sad to leave the store and sad to leave you, Mrs. Zimmerman. You're a great teacher. I do love your son, very much, and I hope you'll see that and welcome me back."

Ephraim followed Laura out of the conference room. As he did so, he noticed Marsha had put her head down on the table and was weeping. For a moment, he was tempted to comfort his mother, but then he thought, she has made her decision and I have made mine.

He helped Laura pack up her few personal belongings and walked her home to her apartment. "I'm sorry for all this, Laura. I always feared this might be her reaction. Will you be able to get another job?"

She looked up at him playfully. "Perhaps I won't. This will give you experience in supporting me. But don't worry. I won't put you to the test yet. A couple of merchants have approached me recently. One wants me to take over his pewter ware store and another would teach me the shoe trade. A job is not the problem. Ephraim, I'm going to be your wife, no matter who objects."

He put an arm around her as they walked. "In the end, no one will object," he said. "You're too lovable. My mother will come around."

They were still two blocks from Laura's apartment when his cell phone rang.

"Freml, what's going on?" Alex asked. "I just got off the phone with my mother and she told me about the incident at the store."

By the time Ephraim explained what had happened, they had reached Laura's apartment building. In the elevator, Ephraim and Laura embraced and kissed. His hands travelled down her back and cupped her buttocks. He felt himself go erect. "Wait," she laughed. "Wait till we get into the apartment."

Once inside, she flung her arms around his neck and walking backwards, led him into her bedroom. Afterwards, they lay comfortably cradled in each others' arms.

"Let's just lie here forever," Ephraim murmured. "I feel so much at peace."

"I'd like that too," Laura said. "But I think you have to see how your mother's doing. She's angry with us but she's hurting and she needs her son. Besides, I believe you can persuade her to accept me. You're not only strong and handsome and smart but you have a way with words. Look what you did to me. All I ever wanted to be was a retailer and now I'm to become a rebbetsyn."

"I don't think it was my words that got you. We just loved."

"We just loved," she agreed.

He was almost dressed, when his cell phone rang. He flipped open the lid without looking at the display, "Ma?"

"No, it's Rebecca. I heard the news on the radio and called the store. Your mother sounded very anxious. Are the police coming up with any clues?"

"Hi, Rebecca," he answered, and watched Laura's head snap around with interest. "So far the only clue is a man seen on the surveillance tape whom the police believe is the culprit. Since his back was towards the camera, it may be impossible to identify him. The incident is quite upsetting for my mother."

"Shouldn't you be there with her? I know she looks to you for support."

Laura was standing in front of him, arms akimbo, a stern look on her face. He reached a hand under her skirt and softly stroked an inner thigh. "I'm on my way to the store now. I'll let you know if the police come up with anything more."

"Well, I like that," Laura said after he hung up. "You hardly get through making love to me and you're talking to my chief rival."

He gathered her in his arms. "She's not your rival, chief or otherwise. I shouldn't tell you that. Jealousy flatters a man."

When he reached the store, Marsha was busy with a customer and she barely nodded at him. He saw that her eyes were bloodshot and some of her eye shadow had dribbled down her cheek. The customer also noticed it because she said sympathetically, "Mrs. Zimmerman, I hope whatever problem you're having is not too serious."

"Not to worry," Marsha replied quickly. "It's a family thing that I believe will sort itself out one way or the other." She shot a significant look at Ephraim.

After the customer left, Ephraim embraced his mother. "Ma, I hate to see you in such pain. It'll all work out. You'll see."

"I don't know, Freml. Right now I feel completely let down. All my hopes for you are gone. Maybe it was foolish of me to dream up an expectation of my son the rabbi, sought after by congregations and schools, supported by a religious wife who brings promising children into the world, a delight to the grandparents. What you and Laura are doing has destroyed the dream. Her mother isn't happy, your mother isn't happy — I suppose you and Laura are happy."

He continued to hold his mother and kissed her forehead. "Ma, we're more than happy — we're ecstatic."

"Is she what caused your doubts about God and our religion?" Marsha demanded.

"Ma, you know I had the doubts long before I met Laura. We Jews have a strong belief in destiny ordained by the Almighty. Like Gertie once said, 'if it's meant to be, it'll happen.' We didn't set out to love each other — it just happened. Ma, please give it a lot of thought and find a way to accommodate us. Even Tevye in *Fiddler* finally acknowledged his daughter who had married the Catholic boy."

"Freml, I'm not going to disown you and ask you to leave the house. You're still my son and you have a mother's love. But I'm sick at heart and need time to heal." She gently pushed Ephraim away. "Now, go do your work at the Institute. I'll be ok."

He was anxious to get back to work. He was leaving for Guernsey the next day and he still had to complete his sermon and review the Torah reading for Saturday. He worked long and hard that afternoon, skipping supper and trying to concentrate on the task at hand. The only leisure he allowed himself was to talk to Laura a couple of times.

He caught the late morning train the next day and was busily revising his sermon when his mother called. "I have a problem," Marsha said without any preamble. "In all the excitement of the last couple of days, I forgot the

International Gift show near the airport runs from Sunday to Wednesday and I need to go. It's the main Christmas buying opportunity. I was counting on Laura to run the store while I'm at the Show. I don't have confidence in the other two staff and they're only part time. I'd like you to call her and ask her to stand in for the four days. What comes after that I don't know. Do you think she will do it or is she too proud?"

Laura readily assented. "Yes, she has to attend. Otherwise, we'll have nothing new to sell and have to get by with a parade of salespeople pushing their products. I had an interview first thing this morning and I was offered the job — it's the one in the shoe store — and can start right away but I'll put it off until Thursday."

"Gosh, you're remarkable," Ephraim said. "Is the pay ok?"

"I'll be on commission. I'll either make nothing or more than you, great and revered rabbi."

He was still chuckling as he hung up and went back to his sermon. He was grateful that Laura took it all in good humour.

At the hotel in downtown Guernsey, he showered and put on his best clothing in preparation for the Sabbath. As he was about to leave for the synagogue, his cell phone buzzed. It was already close to six o'clock and he debated whether he should take the call. If he didn't, then the message would sit there until after the Sabbath.

The display told him it was Rebecca. "Ephraim, I know it's late but I just have to talk to you. I met with Brian Ruby at lunch to go over the story about our school. We got onto the anti-Semitic incident. Brian believes it's not just random because of the message. This morning he returned to the store to talk to the employees and asked for your mother's assistant. Your mother said she'd left. Now Brian is convinced there's more to the story."

"Brian believes he's a great investigative journalist, just a story away from a Pulitzer," Ephraim said, emphasizing the sarcasm in his voice. "Don't try to dissuade him. Laura has taken a couple of days off because she'll have to work four twelve-hour days so my mother can attend the Gift Show. If you check on Sunday, you'll find her happily at work. Anyway, I gotta go. It's not nice for the rabbi to show up late on Friday night."

Why didn't I tell her the truth? Ephraim thought as he walked to the synagogue. The real story is bound to get out soon anyway. All I've done is put Rebecca off. But his mother had advised him to let Rebecca down gently. The telephone was not the way to do it. Better he should meet with her privately, explain the situation, and hope to persuade her to accept him as part of the project. He was still intrigued by the idea of her school and wanted to participate in it. And, despite his love for Laura, he liked Rebecca and relished the thought of working with her.

CHAPTER 9

The Family Is Not Happy

Laura was waiting for him in Union Station on Sunday night. He knew that something was wrong as they embraced and kissed.

"Frowns and no smiles," he said, gently stroking her cheek. "You'll spoil that delicate complexion I've come to love."

"I got a call from Frank earlier this evening. He was ranting and raving about how we're framing him and we won't get away with it. The police picked him up yesterday for questioning. He denies everything, even to being in the mall that night. I told him I know he's guilty, I recognized him on the tape, and to just leave us alone and mind his own business. Then I hung up. Ephraim, sweetheart, I'm worried. He's trouble."

Ephraim held her tightly to him as they walked through the station to the subway. "Let me talk to the policeman who was at the meeting and see what he suggests. If Frank calls you again or continues to bother us, we'll register a complaint. Where does he work?"

Laura shrugged. "I don't really know. He said he was an export/import agent and worked mostly out of his car. He must be doing well because he always had lots of money, mostly cash. He didn't like credit cards."

They were silent as they lined up for the turnstile and pushed through, following the crowd to the Yonge Street platform. On the train, they found two seats close together at the end of the car.

"I know what you're thinking," Laura said. "Lots of cash and no definite place of business. Very suspicious. Yes, I was nervous about him. Ephraim, he was never my boyfriend like you are. I met him only a couple of months before you. He was very polite with me and my mother. He's a strong good looking guy and has a certain European style that I found appealing. He even asked my mother whether he could date me. After you showed up, that's when he began making the racist remarks."

At the Finch end stop, they took the bus up Yonge Street to Steeles and walked from there. By the time Ephraim arrived home, it was midnight, his mother was asleep, and, after saying the Night Prayer, he crawled into bed.

"My boy, it is not too late to alter the course of your life."

The elderly, high-pitched voice of Elijah pierced through the golden haze that enveloped the room. Ephraim saw him sitting on the desk, his robes pulled closely around him. "You invite the forces of evil. The devil sees a weakness and is prepared to strike. Stop now before the damage cannot be reversed. Disaster looms."

Ephraim sat up, propping the pillow behind him. "I do not understand, Eliyahu. My wife-to-be is learning to become Jewish and will shortly join our people. In this, I am obeying Jewish law. I cannot give in to the actions of a man who hates us. Surely, the Almighty will protect me."

Elijah shook his head. "It is the Almighty who has warned you."

Ephraim slid his legs off the bed and sat facing Elijah. "No, Eliyahu, I beg to differ. It was a man consumed by hatred and jealousy who scrawled his message on the store window."

Elijah's laugh was sardonic, dripping with contempt. "My poor boy, do you not realize that the Almighty chooses agents to carry out His work. Abide by the warning. It is not too late."

Ephraim prostrated himself before Elijah. His face buried in the carpet, he pleaded. "No, Eliyahu, it cannot be so. My love is pure. It cannot be against God's will."

"Well may you beg, my boy. It is useless. The severe decree may already be signed and sealed but it can be averted by prayer and penitence. The Israelite woman awaits you. Sever your betrothal to the Midianite. That is all that is required."

Eyes bloodshot, rubbing a stiff neck, Ephraim joined Marsha at breakfast. "You don't look very well," she said to him. "When I went in to wake you, you were lying flat out, face down on the rug. For a terrible moment, I thought you were dead. Something's wrong with you. Is it Laura?"

He took a long swallow of his coffee before replying, savouring the hot liquid in his throat. "No, ma, just a bad dream. How was the gift show?"

Marsha put her cup down sharply. "Don't try to change the subject. I know something is wrong with you. I sometimes hear you talking in your sleep and now you're sleepwalking. You're not well. This Laura thing is getting to you, isn't it?"

Ephraim put down the piece of toast he was eating. "Ma, I love Laura, I want to marry her and I resent all the people standing in our way. I've tried to abide by my religious beliefs. Laura is trying to accommodate me by converting. Why can't everybody accept that we're mature adults, capable of making important decisions?"

Marsha began to cry. "Freml, you mean me, don't you? I'm standing in your way. And your Laura is blameless. My store is decorated with her boy friend's love messages. What nice girl attracts such racist criminals? You can't see it, and there's definitely something wrong with you."

Ephraim pulled his chair around and sat beside his mother, an arm around her shoulder. "Ma, really, I'm ok. Laura is a nice girl. That's why Frank was attracted to her. She befriended him because she felt sorry for him. And she's nice enough to do you a favour and run the store for four days even after you fired her."

Marsha leaned her head on his shoulder. "Yes, Laura is doing me a favour and I do appreciate it. But I can't change my mind so quickly."

Dave Wilson confirmed that he had questioned Frank, but there was nothing they could do to substantiate his guilt. "If Yanovich makes any more contact, let us know and we'll get a restraining order."

Ephraim next met with mall security. Richard Turner promised to increase surveillance of the store. Ephraim called Alex and brought him up to date.

"Sounds like you're having a rough time," Alex said solicitously. "I'm coming over after work and we can talk some more. Just hang in there. Your mother will come around."

Ephraim was looking forward to some time with Alex. His mother would be away at a gift show dinner. He would have liked Laura to join him but she was in the store until nine pm.

Alex arrived around seven and the two sat down to a meal of smoked meat sandwiches and coleslaw. They were sitting back, enjoying a cup of tea when they heard the apartment door open. In walked Marsha, Uncle Avram, Gertie and Irving.

"Freml," Irving said as he headed for the cabinet with the whisky bottles, "I have nothing to do with this. I'm merely following orders. As far as I'm concerned, you can marry anyone you want."

"Irving, just have a drink and shut up," Gertie said, rather shortly. "Freml, your mother's very upset and we've come to talk things over. Alex, I don't know why you'd want to be present at a family discussion."

Alex had risen to greet the arrivals and was in the midst of hugging and kissing Marsha.

"Just a second, Gertie," Ephraim said angrily. "Who are you to throw *my* friends out of *my* house? There's not going to be a family discussion because I don't remember agreeing to have one. Ma, if you want to talk about me and Laura, that's fine but the others have to go."

Marsha, sobbing, grabbed Alex as he was turning away. "Alex, tell him what a mistake he's making. He'll listen to you."

"Marsha, you're going mishuga on us too," Uncle Avram objected. "How can Alex tell him? Alex has committed the same sin."

Alex shrugged. "I didn't realize marrying an opera singer was a sin. Mind you, there are difficulties. She's often away and when she's home, I have to listen to hours of scales."

"Alex, you know exactly what my father means," Gertie said. "Everybody I mention this to cannot understand how a rabbi can marry a shiksa. Rebecca burst into tears when I told her."

"I did that girl a disservice when I introduced you," Uncle Avram exclaimed, waving his arms. "You lied to me. You said you weren't ready for marrying. You weren't ready for marrying Jewish girls, only shiksas."

Ephraim grabbed a flailing arm. "Uncle Avram, when I said that I meant it — I had not yet met Laura or gotten to know her. I sincerely believed it would be years before I'd marry. And one more thing to all of you. Don't refer to my wife-to-be as a shiksa. Her name is Laura. Now that's the end of the discussion. I'm disgusted, Gertie, that you would tell Rebecca. It was my job to tell her, not yours."

"Bravo, Freml," Irving shouted as he downed a shot glass of whisky. "Hey, Alex, let's talk business. What mergers are you working on that I should know about?"

Alex, laughing, walked over to Irving. "If I tell you, it's called insider trading and we'll both go to jail." Alex poured himself a drink and brought one over to Ephraim.

In the meantime, Marsha had sat down on one of the kitchen chairs and was bent over the table, her face in her hands, quietly weeping. "I'm sorry, Freml," she gasped between sobs. "I didn't invite them here. It just seemed to happen."

Ephraim sat down beside her." It's ok, Ma, I'm not angry with you. You're entitled to be upset and to argue with your wayward son. Here, have a sip of my whisky — we'll both feel better."

"This is no problem you can drink away," Uncle Avram proclaimed loudly.

"That's right," Gertie joined in.

"I've always found it helpful," Irving insisted. "Especially when the market tanks."

Gertie pointed an accusing finger at her husband. "Irving, you're not taking this seriously at all."

Irving swallowed another shot of whisky. "What's there to take seriously? A man and a woman, both in their mid to late twenties, decide to marry. We should be celebrating, not mourning. How do we know better? Auntie Marsha, Freml, I raise my glass and wish you l'chaim and say Mazeltov." He began singing the Mazeltov song, drunkenly off key, while he and Alex linked arms and danced in a circle.

"Why did I ever let my daughter marry him?" Uncle Avram exclaimed, raising his eyes to the ceiling.

"Irving! Alex! Stop this nonsense right now," Gertie shouted. "The problem is marrying the shik — marrying Laura will end his career."

"So what," Irving shouted back, still dancing. "It's his lookout. Why are we involved? Hey, Freml, if you can't work as a rabbi, take the Canadian Securities Course and I'll make a stock broker out of you."

"Forget it," Alex said. "There's more money in investment banking."

Ephraim and Marsha stood in the entrance to the living room. Despite their anguish and the gravity of the situation, they couldn't help smiling. Alex and Irving were now facing each other, clapping hands, alternately extending a leg and still circling each other, and bellowing out: "Mazeltov, oi Mazeltov, n' Mazeltov, oi Mazeltov." Gertie was shaking a fist at her husband and Uncle Avram continued to look gloomy and raise his eyes to the ceiling.

EPHRAIM

Over the din of the singing and clapping, Ephraim heard his cell phone ring.

"Hang on, Rebecca," he shouted into the phone. "Let me go to my room."

"What was all that noise?" Rebecca asked as he shut the door to his bedroom. "It sounded like singing." Her voice betrayed no emotion, was studiously flat and cold.

"Some of my relatives are here — watching television."

"Gertie told me something today that I find disturbing. I thought I should check it out directly with you. I understand you're planning to marry a Gentile woman, your mother's shop assistant. Is that correct?"

"Partly correct. She's a Gentile at the moment but is studying to convert. By the time we marry, she'll be Jewish. Look, I'm sorry you had to hear this from Gertie. I should have been the one to discuss it first with you because of the potential impact on the school. However, since I'll be marrying a Jewish girl, you won't have an intermarried rabbi on your faculty."

"You're technically correct," she snapped. "But what will my donors and supporters think? A rabbi who can't exert enough self-discipline to resist the whim of the moment. I want tougher people in my school — people who cherish the spirit of Judaism rather than trying to find ways around it." Her tone had become emotional and heated and her voice cracked as she finished.

Ephraim felt the hurt at the end of the line. He cursed Gertie and Uncle Avram — they had probably stoked her expectations regarding him.

"Rebecca, I'm sorry to disappoint you but I object to you labelling Laura as the whim of the moment. We took time to decide whether marriage between us was even possible. I can't help feeling about her as I do and I don't see why I shouldn't."

There was a long silence. "I'm not going to argue with you but I do question your judgement. Another example — you were wrong in your criticism of Brian Ruby. He guessed correctly that there was something more to the graffiti than a random incident."

"I haven't changed my mind about Ruby," Ephraim said. "Even a broken clock is right twice a day."

"Laugh all you want. He's going to write up the story and it'll hurt your reputation even more. Another reason why I can't hire you. I think you'll have difficulty finding a job as a rabbi. Perhaps if we meet, I can help you. I have lots of contacts in the education field. Some of them might not look too closely at your personal behaviour."

There was a faint plaintive quality to her voice now. She won't give up without a fight, Ephraim thought. He hesitated to meet with her — what would Laura say?

Rebecca didn't wait for an answer and pressed on. "My summertime day camp programme ends at 5:30. We can meet at the Bathurst Community Centre."

He agreed to meet but put it off a full week to the following Monday.

The singing and dancing had stopped when Ephraim rejoined the group. They were sitting quietly on the easy chairs and sofa in the living room. Alex had poured drinks for everyone.

"What did Rebecca have to say?" Gertie asked.

Ephraim ignored the question and sat down beside his mother.

"If you go ahead with this marriage, I shall disown you," Uncle Avram said, straightening up and trying to look dignified and stern. "I shall never talk to you again."

Ephraim was about to make a sarcastic reply but he reminded himself that his uncle was the elder in the family and had to be respected.

"That will be too bad," he said mildly. "I hope in time you will change your mind as you get to know Laura."

"She cannot have a good character," Uncle Avram insisted.

Ephraim felt the anger swelling within him. "Well," he snapped, "if her character is so poor, why is she working in the store so my mother can attend the gift show despite the fact that my mother fired her. Laura is very good-natured with high ethical standards. She wants to be my rebbetsyn and to support me in my work. I'm completely confident that she will. The only thing you know about her and don't like is her religion and she's changing that. The only person I want approval from is my mother. If the rest of you never talk to me again, I'll somehow survive."

Irving and Alex both stood up and applauded.

"I believe the matter is closed," Irving announced. "Let's just socialize or go home."

"Please go home," Marsha pleaded. "I don't mean to be rude but I need some quiet time."

Alex stayed behind after the others left. Ephraim prepared a pot of tea and a plate of cookies and set them on the kitchen table.

"Give me a few minutes," he said. "It's time for Mincha and Maariv."

EPHRAIM

He put extra fervour into the prayers as he recited them in the privacy of his bedroom. In his mind, he sought out the Almighty and beseeched him to bless his love.

"Alex has proposed an outing," Marsha said when he returned to the kitchen. "Polly is singing in Stratford Thursday evening and Alex is suggesting we all go."

"It also does me a favour," Alex admitted. "Polly has our car and is in Stratford all week and won't be coming home until Saturday. My parents are driving around Nova Scotia. So if you take me, I get to watch her perform and to see her before Saturday."

"It's a good idea," Ephraim agreed. "We all need a time out. Ma, I'd like Laura to come with us. Will you be ok with that?"

Marsha took a long time to answer. "I don't know. The idea of an outing was to get away for an evening and to forget all our troubles."

"Ma, I'll discuss it with Laura. But don't put me in a position where I have to tell one of the two women I most love in this world to stay home."

It was Laura who decided not to go. "I start my new job on Thursday — to go to Stratford means leaving mid-afternoon. Besides, my Jewish course is Thursday evening and now that you're meeting with my rival, I want to convert as fast as possible to get you out of her reach."

They were sitting side by side at the back of the bar they usually frequented. The area was dark except for the guttering candle light on each table.

Ephraim nuzzled her ear. "Rebecca is not your rival and we're meeting to go over job contacts."

Laura leaned her head on his shoulder. "Sweetest of rabbis, we both know why she wants to meet with you. The reason I don't object is because you're a rabbi and you have to throw some balm her way. I know that, as part of your job, you'll occasionally meet with good-looking distressed women seeking help. Just remember — your guidance is spiritual, not sexual. That you keep for the good-looking distressed woman at home."

He threw back his head and laughed. "Is that what they're teaching in your course? I better examine the curriculum."

The DJ returned from his break and the music started up. A rotating light cast flickering shadows on the postage-sized dance floor in front of the six-seater bar.

Laura pulled him off the padded bench. "C'mon. We need some exercise."

They held each other for a moment, moving rhythmically with the music. They pushed apart. Ephraim quick stepped while Laura swayed and popped her hips, gyrating and twisting. She was wearing a short skirt. In the sporadic, rolling light, he caught tantalizing glimpses of calf and thigh.

A large body loomed out of the semi-darkness and a beefy hand pushed Ephraim aside.

"I dance now."

Laura stopped dancing, put her hands on her hips and said defiantly: "Frank, leave us alone. I don't want to dance with you."

Despite the summer heat, Frank was wearing a double breasted suit. A silk tie hung loosely from a limp white collar.

"Why you no dance with me? Why him?" he demanded as he thrust a contemptuous thumb in Ephraim's direction.

"Because we are soon to be married."

Frank looked at her incredulously. "You marry him?"

Laura nodded. Frank turned and grasped Ephraim by the scruff of his open neck shirt. "You steal her from me."

Ephraim kept his voice even and calm. "Frank, I'm not going to fight with you. Leave us alone or I'll call the police."

A heavy set man at the bar came over to them. As large as Frank, he was dressed in a black T-shirt and slacks.

"What seems to be the problem, folks?" he asked.

Frank turned on him. "Not your business. Fock off."

"Sorry, it is my business, it's my job. I'm the security guy. The club doesn't like fights or arguments. If the lady doesn't want to dance with you, that's it."

A short thin man sporting a full moustache and also wearing a double breasted suit appeared beside Frank. "We gotta go, Frank," he said.

Frank turned angrily on him. "Why we gotta go? I want dance."

The two began arguing in a language that Ephraim guessed was Russian. Finally Frank said: "Ok, ok, ok."

"We go," the short man said. "We need taxi."

"Not a problem." The security man signalled to the bartender who immediately picked up a telephone. "We have a direct line so the taxi will be here in seconds." He escorted them out of the club.

When Ephraim and Laura were ready to leave, the security man walked them to their car in the parking lot behind the club and waited until they had driven off.

Late the next morning, Ephraim met with Detective Wilson. They sat on a bench in the entrance lobby at the Vaughan Division police station. He recounted the events of the previous night. "Obviously, Frank is following us around. I don't believe it was coincidence that we ended up in the same club."

"Like I said at our meeting in Turner's office, Frank Yanovich is known to us," Wilson said. "So is the short guy that was with him — Lev Medvedev. Both are involved with a local drug gang. They're not kingpins — just enforcers. The gang doesn't like its members attracting attention. That's probably what Lev was telling Frank and why Frank backed down. The two may also be armed. The double breasted suits hide the guns. We'll keep a stronger eye on Frank although I believe the gang has told him to concentrate on business."

Laura was waiting for him outside the Clarke Street synagogue as he emerged after evening prayers. The last grey light of dusk was rapidly disappearing but a gibbous moon hanging in a clear sky illuminated the night. Ephraim kissed her on the lips.

"You're throwing caution to the winds," she exclaimed, "kissing me in front of everybody. Not that I'm complaining."

He held her tightly to him as they walked toward Hilda and her apartment.

"I've given up trying to keep us secret. It's not fair to you — it only serves me. I had a long talk with the Nitskys this afternoon. I told them the woman I love and want to marry is a Gentile but is studying to convert. I apologized for not being wholly truthful with Sholom. They asked a lot of questions about you. Sholom concluded that I'd start on the Nova Scotia job since it was less than a month away, but whether I kept it would depend on you. If your conversion is successful, he'll stay with me."

Laura stopped abruptly and confronted him. They stood facing each other as strollers out enjoying the sultry evening air flowed around them.

"So the whole burden is on me."

He reached out and cupped her chin in his hand. "Sweetheart, there's no burden on you. If you convert, I'm assured of a job as a rabbi. If not, I'll find something else to do. No matter what, I love you, I'll marry you."

They resumed walking, arms around each other. "Not to worry," Laura said. "I rather enjoy the course though some of the rules strike me as over the top. Do you realize, when we have sex, it has to be in a completely darkened room. You've broken the rules. We made love in lit rooms and saw each other's bodies."

"I never looked."

She giggled and squeezed his waist. At the apartment building she invited him up. "My mother's out at her weekly card game. We'll have about an hour to be totally alone."

They embraced and tongued as they rode up in the elevator. He followed her into the apartment and grasped her from behind, his hands cupping her breasts. He was rewarded with an ecstatic moan. He dragged her into her bedroom, lifted her onto the bed, and lay down beside her. Afterwards they lay on their backs, side by side, savouring the delicious sense of release after love-making.

"That was good even in the dark," Laura said. They hadn't turned the lights on in the bedroom.

Soon, he began kissing her. She put a hand over his mouth. "Don't get me all roused up again. My mother will be home soon."

Mrs. Burton arrived and found them at the table in the small dining room off the kitchen having tea and cookies. She smiled at Ephraim and seemed genuinely pleased to see him. He stood up and kissed her on both cheeks. Laura poured her a cup of tea.

"Laura, a friend of yours called me just before I was leaving for my card game. Sounded very upset. Asked me whether I knew you were getting married?"

"Frank?"

Mrs. Burton nodded. "I told him you were very much in love and the man you would marry is very nice. He made some comments about Ephraim that I found offensive and told him to stop such horrible talk. He asked me whether I was happy with you marrying Ephraim and I said absolutely — they're good for each other. That was the end of the conversation. He didn't even say goodbye. Just hung up."

Ephraim put down his teacup. "Sorry you had to have such a phone call. Frank can't seem to leave it alone. Mind you, I understand him in a way. I'm obsessed with Laura. I'd be very upset if someone took her away from me."

"You didn't take me from Frank. I went willingly," Laura objected.

"Ephraim," Mrs. Burton added, "even if you were upset, I can't see you marking up store windows or starting fights in night clubs."

He thought of Mrs. Burton as he walked home along Steeles Avenue. Her acceptance of him had been grudging at first, but now she seemed to relish the idea of him becoming her son-in-law. He hoped his own mother would soon show as much enthusiasm for Laura.

On Thursday, Ephraim was having lunch with the Nitskys in Sholom's office when his cell phone rang.

"I sold my first pair of shoes a few minutes ago," an excited Laura exulted. "My new boss is very impressed and wants me to attend a day long seminar on the shoe industry. It includes a visit to the Bata Shoe Museum."

"Fantastic, Laura. I'm so happy for you."

"But I still would prefer working with your mother," Laura went on. "She was so nice to me — hugged and kissed me every time I came to work. I do hope we get it together again."

"Don't worry," he assured her. "It'll all work out."

CHAPTER 10

The Enemy Strikes Again

Marsha picked him up outside the Chevra Kadisha Institute and then drove downtown to the financial district. Alex was waiting for them at the corner of Bay and Adelaide Streets.

Traffic out of the city was heavy but flowed and allowed them to reach Stratford by six pm. They met Polly in the lobby of the hotel where she was staying — a short walk from Stratford's Festival Hall.

"I've only a half-hour," Polly said after she and Alex had embraced and smothered each other in a long kiss. "I've ordered sandwiches for you — Swiss cheese and lettuce which Alex says you can eat, Ephraim. I won't join you. I'm always too nervous before a performance to eat."

"I thought the Stratford Festival was strictly Shakespeare and other plays. I didn't realize they also have concerts," Marsha said.

"Not usually, Mrs. Zimmerman," Polly explained. "I and other singers are doing a two day fundraiser for the Festival and the Opera Company. We're sold out both nights."

Backstage after the concert, they congratulated Polly.

"You were the best," Marsha gushed, clearly elated.

"I don't know whether I was the best," Polly said. "I know I sang well. I felt inspired by the fact my husband was sitting in the audience."

Polly changed and they all walked back to the hotel. "Now you can buy me dinner," Polly said to Alex.

They watched her put away a steak and mashed potatoes. Ephraim ordered a bottle of wine but Marsha insisted on sticking with coffee. "I'll be the designated driver."

"Before you go," Polly said to Alex. "I need you to look over a contract the Opera Company wants me to sign."

Alex dutifully followed his wife to her hotel room. When he returned, a half-hour later, Ephraim asked him: "Was the contract ok?"

"Contract?" Alex said, a faraway look in his eyes. Ephraim chuckled, but Marsha merely smiled.

It was after midnight when they finally left the hotel and headed toward Toronto. Once out of Stratford, the street lights stopped. Low scudding clouds shielded the moon. The occasional farmhouse cast tiny points of light in the otherwise dark night.

Alex, in the back seat, promptly fell asleep. Ephraim, in the passenger seat beside Marsha, felt his eyelids drooping, weighed down by the wine and the hour. He fought against the drowsiness so he could stay awake, talk to Marsha, and keep her alert.

"That was the first time you met Polly," Ephraim said. "She's quite impressive."

"Yes, beauty, charm and talent. Just like Laura. But I haven't changed my mind."

They passed the village of Shakespeare and proceeded once more into the darkness. The road was two lanes for another ten miles before it expanded into a four lane highway and eventually connected with the expressway home.

Headlights illuminated the interior of the Cadillac as a car came up behind them. Ephraim, sitting sideways in his seat facing Marsha, watched idly as the overtaking car pulled out to pass and then jerked sharply back into the lane.

"There's a car without headlights passing us," Marsha began and then shrieked, "What's he doing?"

In the split second Ephraim saw the dark shape beside them, he heard and felt the screech and crunch of metal on metal. The Cadillac careened off the road, jumped a shallow ditch, whipped around as it hit a tree and then rolled over and over down a sloping lawn and smashed up against a stone gate pillar. The car lay on the driver's side down. Smoke poured from the engine.

The air bags which had deployed now deflated. For the moment dazed, Ephraim hung suspended by his seat belt. A red hue suffused the lower clouds of smoke.

"The car's on fire. We've got to get out," he shouted.

He released his belt and almost fell on Marsha who was screaming hysterically. Twisting frantically, he put a foot on the steering column and pushed up against the passenger door and threw it open. He reached down, released Marsha's seat belt and pulled her out of the seat. With his arms around Marsha, his feet on the steering column and seat backs, he strained upward until his head and shoulders were out of the car. He hoisted Marsha onto the car and then pushed hard until he was sitting beside her. Holding her in his arms, he swivelled around, slid off the car and raced across the lawn. Marsha had stopped screaming and was moaning "What's happening?" over and over. He put his mother down gently and ran back to the car.

Farmhouse lights came on and illuminated the scene. A voice near the road shouted," Hey, buddy, I saw it all. Get away from the car. It's gonna blow."

"My friend," Ephraim screamed, "he's still in there."

He climbed onto the car and threw open the back door. The engine was now a roaring furnace of flame and the heat was intense. The fire burst through the dashboard and lit up the interior of the car. He lay flat and reached inside. Alex lay in a heap on the downside.

The voice shouted again, "For chrissake, buddy, get the hell outta there. She's gonna blow."

He leaned well into the car, barely keeping his balance. He got fingers around Alex's pant belt and pulled. He reached in with his other arm and got a hand under Alex's shoulder. He heaved and pushed back at the same time. The heat was barely tolerable, the flames licking away at the interior of the car. He pulled Alex out of the car and slid with him to the ground. Holding Alex under his shoulders, Ephraim dragged him away. There was a sudden roar and blast of white hot light. He was thrust backward and down and lay in a field of dancing flame. He fought off the deepening blackness that was creeping over him, got to his knees still holding Alex tightly, and felt himself pulled away.

A distant voice cried, "I got you, buddy."

For a brief moment, he sensed the coolness of the night air. Then the gathering darkness engulfed him.

Shafts of deep grey slanted across blackness, pulsating at times like a heartbeat. Gradually the blackness evaporated and the shafts of deep grey alternated with strips of pale grey. Soon the pulsing slowed, stopped and became an effluvium of soupy fog. For what seemed like ages, the fog persisted and then slowly dissipated.

Ephraim opened his eyes and shut them again as the pain of light shocked him.

A stentorian female voice announced: "Your name is Ephraim Zimmerman. You are in Sacred Grace Hospital in Toronto. You are recovering from a car accident."

Ephraim Zimmerman? Car accident? What's she talking about?

It took him a long time to open his eyes and keep them open. He was lying in a bed. He moved an arm, swung a hand into his field of vision and saw the hand was bandaged. He moved his other hand to where he could see it. It too was bandaged but the fingers were clear. He touched his face and felt more bandages. Clearly something dreadful had happened. He struggled to remember.

A face filled his vision — a man's face, round, bushy-browed, white moustache, owl like glasses. "Hi, Rabbi Zimmerman, I'm Dr. Simcoe, head of the burn unit at Grace. You suffered some pretty serious burns but you're going to be ok. To help the healing process, we've kept you in an induced coma for a few weeks. If you're in pain, let the nurses know and they'll look after you."

"Don't remember," Ephraim mumbled and dozed off.

When he opened his eyes again, another face floated into his field of vision: a woman's face, smiling tenderly, eyes awash with tears, coiffed hair framing a remarkably unlined and attractive face. The face was familiar — he had seen it many times — somehow he knew it was his mother.

"Freml, I'm so happy you're going to be alright. I prayed every day and God has blessed us."

Freml? The name evoked a memory of a small boy a long time ago. His parents called him Ephraimele but he pronounced it Freml and the name stuck. And then in a rush of recollection, he remembered who he was.

He reached out a bandaged hand and touched the face. "Ma, something bad happened. How did I get like this?"

She held his hand gently. He noticed a sling held one of her arms. "There was a car accident."

"I don't remember. Were you in the accident too? You're hurt."

"Just a broken arm. I'll soon be all better. We'll talk about the accident some other time."

He dozed off again. This time when he awoke, he could see beyond his bed. Daylight poured into the room through a large window, its Venetian shade pulled up. Two nurses were attending to him, adjusting the bags and instruments that hung on the two poles behind him, and the tubes and wires that disappeared under his covers.

They left and a young woman stood beside his bed. A pretty woman with straight brown hair that fell to her shoulders, brilliant eyes and pouting lips. He felt an immediate tug of affection and desire. She leaned over and kissed him on his forehead.

"Sweetheart," she sobbed, "I'm so sorry this has happened. I feel like it's all my fault. I love you so much. I want you better. That's all that matters."

"Hello," Ephraim said his voice cracked and guttural. "I seem to know you."

Laura stared down at him in shocked surprise. "Sweetheart, you don't remember me? Laura? Laura Burton?"

"Not right now, but it's all coming back. I know my name. I remember my childhood and high school. Even as I'm thinking now, I'm remembering more. It seems to me I studied at Yeshiva U in New York. The doctor called me a rabbi, so I must have graduated. How do I know you?"

"We were planning to marry. You told me many times how much you love me."

He reached out a hand which she grasped. "And I'm sure I'll soon remember everything. Don't worry. If I promised to marry you, I'll marry you."

She kissed the unbandaged fingers of his hand. "But I want you to love me just like before the accident."

He twisted restlessly in his bed. "I'm in terrible pain. Please call the nurse."

The nurse hung a small bag on the intravenous pole and joined it to the drip line. Laura held his hand until the pain began to subside.

"I don't remember the accident. Tell me what happened," he mumbled and fell asleep.

He awoke hours later. The window was dark, the room lit by a neon light behind his bed. A young woman came into the room and stood beside his bed. She was even prettier than his previous visitor. Blonde hair, voluptuous figure. I must be some kind of Don Juan, Ephraim thought, to get visits from such pretty girls. Alex will be envious. Alex? There was something important to remember about Alex but it eluded him. Anyway, Alex no longer chased after girls. He was married now — Polly, an opera singer. Yes, it was all slowly coming back.

"Ephraim, it's me, Rebecca. I'm so happy you survived and you're going to be well again. We were all so worried about you."

He looked at her blankly. "I'm sorry. I know I've seen you before but I don't quite remember who you are."

"You don't remember me?" She began to weep. "Perhaps it's just as well that you don't remember me. I was so mean to you. I came to apologize."

"How do we know each other?"

She leaned over and kissed his forehead. "We met at your cousin Gertie's house. I'm working on a project — a school I'm planning to open and you were helping me and offered to teach in it."

He held up a bandaged arm. "I'll be happy to teach in your school, but who knows how long it'll be before I'm in shape to do it."

Rebecca was silent for a moment. "Well, it'll be a while yet for the school. It's something we can talk about when you're better. I suppose Laura's been in to see you."

Despite the pain that clogged his mind, he detected something artful in her last statement. He nodded.

Any further conversation was interrupted by a nurse who announced that visiting hours were over and she had to prepare Ephraim for the night. Rebecca kissed him again on the forehead and left.

Over the next several days, he was helped off the bed and with a nurse on either side walked first to the door of his room and then out into the hallway. His bandages were changed. The pain was considerable and because of the pain killers, he slept in between treatments and walkabouts.

He was visited frequently by his mother, Laura and Rebecca. Although the three women spoke to each other, he noted a coolness between his mother and Rebecca on one side and Laura on the other. He felt he knew why but couldn't remember. He found himself powerfully attracted to Laura and eagerly awaited her visits.

One morning Laura arrived early. It was a brilliant day. The sun streamed into the room. "I brought you a skull cap and a siddur for the High Holidays," she announced. "You probably have no idea what date this is. Today is Yom Kippur — I know you can't fast but I thought you would like to pray."

He looked at her in astonishment. "Are we that far into September?"

She nodded. "They kept you in a coma for four weeks. You woke up on Rosh Hashanah. It's been ten days since you awoke."

"I'm a rabbi and I missed the holiest period in the Jewish calendar. Tell me, your name — Laura Burton — it doesn't sound Jewish. Are you Jewish?"

She looked away worriedly. Then she gazed directly into his eyes. "Not yet. I'm studying to convert. You said you'd marry me, no matter what but I decided I wanted to be part of your rabbinical life."

He took the skullcap and prayer book. "Well, you're certainly living up to your decision. Does my mother approve?"

Laura helped him put the skull cap on. "Not at the moment. You believe she will come around and accept me."

"What about Rebecca? She's barely civil to you when both of you are here."

"Rebecca doesn't approve either but it's not just religious —I know she had designs on you herself."

Ephraim sighed. "Here I am the object of a love triangle, and I'm too beat up to take advantage."

She leaned over him, kissed his forehead, his nose, the burn scars on his cheeks, and his lips. "You better behave. Now it's time for prayer."

"One more question. Were we intimate?'

She smiled. "Yes, you're pretty good."

He opened the prayer book. "The Yom Kippur service goes on most of the day. I'm not strong enough for that but there are a few prayers that need saying. Help me sit on the edge of the bed and you sit beside me."

They read the prayers together, he in Hebrew, she from the English translation on the alternate page. They were still at it when Dr. Simcoe came in followed by several interns and nurses.

"Sorry to disturb you but it's time for rounds. If the young lady will wait outside."

After a lengthy examination, Ephraim was helped off the bed and sat in a chair. Laura rejoined him.

"You're healing remarkably well," Dr. Simcoe said. "But we still have a number of skin grafts to do."

Laura pulled a chair beside Ephraim and for another hour, they read prayers from the Yom Kippur service. Finally, Ephraim pleaded fatigue and she helped him back into bed. He promptly fell asleep.

EPHRAIM

Laura returned in the early evening and they read together some of the closing prayers. Ephraim enjoyed sitting beside her and was comforted by her presence. He put an arm around her waist, pulled her close and pressed a cheek against hers.

"You're awfully raspy," she said, laughing delightedly. "Your beard has grown around your burn scars. I'll bring an electric razor tomorrow."

He was sitting in a chair beside his bed when she arrived the next morning. A brilliant September sun filled the room with soft autumn light. She draped a towel around his shoulders and carefully applied the razor. She had just finished shaving Ephraim when Marsha arrived with Uncle Avram, Irving, Gertie, and Rebecca. Ephraim noticed the sudden tension between Laura and the others. His mother greeted Laura politely, the others said nothing, except Irving who came over, introduced himself and shook her hand. They were loud and long in their greeting of Ephraim.

"Freml," Uncle Avram said, grasping both Ephraim's hands. "I can't tell you how much we've prayed for you, hoping that God would allow us the blessing of having you among us again. Your mother cried every night you were in the coma. Only now is she relaxed. And Rebecca here has some good news for you but she can tell you herself."

"Ephraim," Rebecca said, "I'm starting a campaign early next year to raise money for the school. I'd like you to help me and also take a hand in running the school and teaching in it. All you have to do is get better fast."

"Amen," said Gertie. "That's what we all wish."

"We couldn't come yesterday to see you because it was Yom Kippur," Uncle Avram explained. "But I guess you were unaware of the days and didn't realize it."

"I wasn't aware until Laura brought me a kippa and a siddur and we said some of the prayers together. I was amazed at how long I've been here."

Irving burst out laughing. "That's cool — Laura did Yom Kippur with you. Good for you, Laura."

"Irving, that's enough," Gertie said.

"That's right," Uncle Avram agreed, wagging an angry finger at his son-in-law. "It's not funny. She's the reason Freml is here."

Laura kissed Ephraim. "I'll see you later when they're gone."

Irving stopped her from leaving. "Papa, that's not fair. You can't blame Laura for the act of an insanely jealous thug," he objected.

"Irving's right, Avram," Marsha said.

"Would somebody explain what this is all about," Ephraim pleaded. "I remember nothing about the accident. The last thing I remember with any clarity is the day I arrived home from New York. There are bits and pieces after that but it's mostly hazy."

They were silent for a moment. "Dearest," Marsha said, "the Doctor has asked us not to talk about the accident until you're better. At the moment, it may be too difficult for you to handle."

"But, Ma, you're all accusing Laura of causing the accident. That already stresses me out."

"Why should that cause you stress?" Uncle Avram demanded, glaring at his nephew. "You don't even remember her."

He had moved forward to make his point and Marsha pushed him back. "Avram, you're not helping."

Ephraim was clearly angry as he snapped back. "The details of Laura before the accident may be lost to me right now, but I accept that I asked her to marry me and I do have feelings for her. It bothers me that, except for Irving, you're all hostile to her. If you're worried about my stress level, you're all raising it."

"Please, sweetheart, don't get upset," Laura said, gently stroking his cheek.

Ephraim relaxed and sat back in his chair. "Explain why you think Laura's at fault."

Irving stepped forward and sat on the edge of the bed facing Ephraim. "Laura is not at fault and had nothing to do with the accident. The guy who caused the accident is Frank Yanovich. Does the name mean anything to you?"

Ephraim shook his head.

"Yanovich believes Laura is his girlfriend and you stole her away. Not only that, Yanovich is a rabid anti-Semite and he couldn't accept losing his girl to a Jew. So he did things to hurt you and to intimidate Laura. He wrote anti-Semitic graffiti on your mother's store. He tried to start a fight with you in a nightclub but a security guard kicked him out."

"I'm sorry," Ephraim said. "I remember nothing of this. What about the accident?"

"What happened comes from the police," Irving continued. "You and Auntie Marsha and Alex drove to Stratford to attend a concert featuring Polly,

EPHRAIM

Alex's wife in case you don't remember. Yanovich saw the Cadillac leave the Esplanade mall parking lot and followed. He saw Auntie Marsha pick you up and then Alex. Yanovich was driving a Hummer and he had with him his sidekick — a guy by the name of Lev Medvedev. According to Lev's confession, he objected but Yanovich insisted on following you, all the way to Stratford. They fell behind a few cars when they got to Stratford and missed seeing you pull into the hotel. They drove around for a long time. They stopped for dinner. Finally, Yanovich had given up the hunt and was driving back when he spotted you all getting into the Cadillac as he passed the hotel. Lev thought Yanovich only wanted to scare you but claims he was horrified when Yanovich forced you off the road and damaged the Hummer at the same time.

"A witness observed the accident and stopped to help. The car was on fire and lying on its side. Ephraim, you pulled Auntie Marsha out and then went back for Alex. You got Alex out and then the car blew.

"A short time after, a policeman stopped a Hummer speeding on the 401

"The policeman also noticed the damage on the passenger side. To make a long story short, they eventually tied the Hummer to the accident. Medvedev readily confessed but Yanovich fled back to Russia. The police here don't think they'll ever get him."

"Wow, that's quite a story," Ephraim said.

Marsha rubbed a hand through his hair. "You were very brave, my dear, pulling us out. The man who stopped to help said the car was a mass of flame."

"How's Alex?" Ephraim asked. "He must have been burnt as well."

"Alex is ok," Irving said quickly.

"What do you mean he's ok," Avram interjected. "Has no one told him the truth?" — Marsha tried to stop him, putting a hand over his mouth, but he brushed it away — "Your friend died on the way to hospital."

There was a stunned silence. They all looked at Ephraim.

Ephraim rose from his chair, staring wildly around the room. "No!" he shrieked. "No! No! No! You're all liars! Liars! Liars!"

He began to tear off his bandages. Laura flung her arms around him. "Don't! Please don't!" They both sank to the floor, sobbing, Ephraim still shouting "No!"

An intern ran in, followed by a nurse. "What the hell's going on? What are you doing to my patient? Get the hell outta here, all of you."

No one moved. The intern pushed brusquely through, and spat out a command to the nurse. She ran out and returned quickly, brandishing a hypodermic needle, which she plunged into Ephraim's arm. Within seconds, he stopped shouting and his head fell forward.

"Miss, let him go," the intern said to Laura. He and the nurse manipulated Ephraim onto his bed. The nurse redid the bandages.

"I asked you to leave," the intern said. "Or do I have to call Security."

"This is my nephew and I have every right to visit him. He's upset because everybody kept the truth from him."

"Avram, shut up," Marsha snapped angrily.

"Auntie Marsha, that's no way to talk to my father," Gertie objected. "He meant well."

"Your father's an idiot. He hurt my son."

Avram hung his head sheepishly. "Marsha, I'm sorry. I wasn't thinking."

"Ladies and gentlemen," the intern said. "I have a sick patient here whom you've made sicker. We have a lovely cafeteria on the ground floor. There you can sort out your family problems, not here. My patient is tranquilized but can hear everything you say. He's had enough trauma for one day."

Laura was still sitting on the floor, weeping quietly. The intern helped her up. "There, there, miss. He'll be alright. Just needs some peace and quiet."

"Doctor," a faint, slurred voice emanated from the bed. "Let my mother and Laura stay. I need to talk to them."

The intern was reluctant at first but finally relented. "OK, ladies, but if he starts getting excited, out you go."

"Mrs. Zimmerman," Rebecca said, "I'll wait for you in the lobby and drive you home."

They trooped out of the room — Avram with his head down, Gertie glaring angrily, Irving shaking his head, Rebecca waving to Ephraim and throwing him a kiss. Ephraim raised a hand feebly and waved back.

Ephraim's voice was very faint. Both women had to lean over him to hear.

"Ma, Laura, is it all true?"

Both women nodded.

"Alex was like a brother. We should have died together."

Marsha and Laura both protested but kept their voices gentle.

"What about the Feldmans? Polly?"

"It was a great shock to the Feldmans," Marsha said. "It'll take a while for them to recover."

"The same for Polly," Laura added.

"Eliyahu warned me." Ephraim muttered, sighing. "I didn't listen. I loved Laura too much." He closed his eyes and drifted off into a deep sleep.

CHAPTER 11

Travels In Ancient Egypt

The blackness was pushed aside by a golden haze that illuminated the dimly lit room. Ephraim opened his eyes. His mother and Laura were gone. Confronting him was the tall white-bearded figure of Elijah. The Prophet looked sadly but sympathetically at him.

"Why?" Ephraim asked and did not try to hide the anger and bitterness in his voice. "Why my friend? Why not me?"

Elijah leaned over the bed and put a reassuring hand on Ephraim's head but Ephraim shook it off.

"My boy, do not be cross with me. I am but the messenger. Why? It is impossible to know why. We cannot divine or understand the Almighty's decisions and acts. Suffice it to say — you have sinned and the Almighty has punished. Be satisfied that the Almighty spared you and your mother. It is good that He spared your mother. She will help guide you back to a life of righteousness. The woman of Israel awaits you — forsake the Midianite."

Ephraim sat up in his bed and swung his legs over the side, forcing Elijah to step back. "I do not agree that I have sinned. My marriage to Laura — to the Midianite — was months away and by then she would have become an Israelite."

Elijah shook his head. "My boy, we prophets can only glimpse the future but the Almighty sees it clearly. He sees all the paths you might take through life to the end of your days. He has warned you that an alliance with the Midianite does not favour you as a priest and leader of our people. Even I can perceive that you will stray under the influence of the Midianite. Your carnal lust will rob you of sound judgement. Take heed."

Ephraim shrugged and lay back in the bed. "Eliyahu, with all respect, I cannot accept that. My love for the Midianite is pure. It is love of her that drives me, not merely lust. I do not wish to know other women. What then is my sin?"

"The Lord has directed you to follow a certain path and you are prepared to ignore His wise counsel. In this you are perpetrating sin and you will continue in sin. You have angered the Almighty."

A figure entered the room and stood at the end of Ephraim's bed. "Freml, don't listen to him," the figure said.

Ephraim sat up and stared into the golden haze. A short, round faced man with a mischievous grin, looking and sounding like Alex came into focus.

"You've done nothing wrong," Alex said. "The next thing he'll tell you is I sinned by marrying Polly."

"Exactly so," Elijah agreed.

Tears streamed down Ephraim's face as he reached out to his friend. "Alex, I'm so sorry, so terribly sorry. Please forgive me."

Alex waved a deprecating hand. "Nothing to forgive. It wasn't your fault. Don't apologise for some psycho asshole. And don't believe it's retribution for some sin. Bullshit. Your Prophet's balls dried up a long time ago. He couldn't begin to understand real love and our modern world. Tell him to get lost."

Ephraim was shocked. "Alex, you're talking to Eliyahu Hanavi."

The Prophet drew himself up and wrapped his cloak tightly around him, as though warding off the evil flowing from the end of the bed. "Mind him not, my son. In my lifetime I endured much censure from my enemies but my prophecies prevailed. It is in the nature of my ministry that I remind all men that their acts are not isolated but ramify well beyond them. What a man may believe is a minor misdemeanour of little consequence will have unforeseen repercussions. He who is rebellious of the Almighty will cause hardship not only to himself but to those around him."

Alex snorted disdainfully. "In life, good things happen, bad things happen. Who's to say why? Sure, things people do or decide have unintended consequences. That's because the world is a terribly complex place and nobody can quite predict all its intricacies. Two tectonic plates rub against each other, cause an earthquake and a tsunami and 200,000 people die. Was God behind this? Were these people all sinners? Or are we supposed to believe He took them all out because he was unhappy with a few? C'mon Prophet, get real."

Elijah seemed unperturbed by Alex's disparaging and rude remarks. He turned to Ephraim. "My son, abide not your friend's false understanding. Come. Let us observe the first of your name and the fortunes of the tribe Ephraim."

Ephraim was not aware they had left the hospital but suddenly they stood at the edge of a large valley bathed in brilliant sunshine. The valley sloped downward to a meandering brook and rose again to join the mountains on the other side. Herds of sheep, goats, oxen, camels, and donkeys cropped the luscious green that spread out before them. Here and there, a herdsman with a long crooked staff walked amongst them, although nothing seemed to menace the utter pastoral peace of the scene.

Close by was a large tent, its side panels raised to let in a slight breeze. In the tent, an old man, bald and gaunt, lay on a bed, his head propped up with pillows. He was naked except for a length of cloth that covered his loins. A sparse white beard sprinkled his chin and cheeks. Several women hovered round the bed, occasionally massaging his forehead with a rag dipped in a bowl of water.

Outside the tent, a crowd of men and women stood around or squatted on the ground. All wore long cloaks, except some of the men who were stripped to the waist and wore a leather skirt. The keening of the women was loud and constant. The men bowed their heads but said nothing while some wept unashamedly.

"What's going on?" Alex asked.

"We are in the land of Goshen, in Egypt," Elijah replied. "Jacob, the last of our forefathers, is on his deathbed."

Across the valley, three fast moving horses came into view, their riders leaning forward, lashing the horses' haunches with short whips. They leapt across the brook and barrelled through the grazing herds, scattering them wildly, bleating and baying.

The three horsemen stopped well short of the tent. The lead man was tall, muscular, dressed in a short tunic, naked to the waist except for a leather belt that ran diagonally across his chest and over a shoulder. A short black beard jutted out from his jaw but he was otherwise clean shaven.

Ephraim guessed the two with him, similarly dressed but without beards, were teenagers. The three pulled off their calf high riding boots and walked barefoot to the tent. They embraced and greeted the men waiting there. A woman placed a bowl of water before them and washed their feet. Another woman handed them a goatskin gourd and they each drank in turn.

A young woman came out of the tent and bowing, said: "He asks for Joseph."

Joseph motioned to the two boys to follow him and went to Jacob's bedside. "Father, I am here and with me are my two sons, Manasseh and Ephraim."

Servants assisted Jacob to sit up. Joseph held Jacob's hand and kissed it.

"My hand is wet with your tears, my son. Do not weep. My time has come but my life has been full. We owe much to you — we prosper because of you and because of the Almighty Who works through you. And for this reason, I declare your two sons shall be as mine."

Joseph pushed the two boys forward. They kneeled in front of Jacob.

"My eyes are clouded," Jacob said. "Place my hands on their heads."

Joseph put Jacob's right hand on Manasseh and his left hand on Ephraim. Jacob reversed the order and placed his right hand on Ephraim and his left on Manasseh.

"Nay, my father, Manasseh is the older and should receive the birthright."

Jacob shook his head. "My son, my eyes fail me here but perceive the time to come. Both your sons will be great but Ephraim will be greater."

Jacob looked down at the two boys. "My children, the Almighty has blessed me all my life and fed me right up to this moment. I pass this blessing onto you, Ephraim and Manasseh, and say unto you — walk in the path of the Almighty and as He directs and you will prosper." He leaned over, restrained by Joseph from falling out of the bed, and kissed the two boys.

Joseph and his sons prostrated themselves before Jacob and, all three weeping, backed slowly out of the tent.

Ephraim found himself back in bed, Elijah at his bedside, Alex at the foot. Ephraim's eyes were wet with tears.

"Eliyahu, that was very moving. It brought to mind my own father's death. He left us so suddenly I never had the chance to say goodbye nor to receive his blessing. I do remember the advice he gave me when I left for New York. 'Always do what you think is right. Follow the dictates of your conscience.' I believe that's what I'm doing. I have studied and learned the commandments of the Almighty and I try to observe them. What more can I or any man of our faith do?"

"That's it, Freml. Stand up to him. You're doing the best you can in a difficult world."

Elijah looked mournfully at Alex. "Poor soul, your counsel is flawed. The Almighty demands strict observance. There are 613 commandments in our sacred Torah. These are not like the pits of the pomegranate where you can eat some and spit others out. All must be eaten. That is the path the Almighty has revealed to the children of Israel. There is no other path, no compromises, no half-measures. And that is the path the first Ephraim took."

Ephraim considered Elijah's words carefully. In the Prophet's view, his love of Laura was considered a deviation from the word of God. Yet Joseph was blessed and he had married the daughter of a priest of Egypt. But Joseph had had no choice in the matter — Ephraim had choice.

"Eliyahu," he said, "I know the tribe did well, particularly after the Israelites entered Canaan. Was this because of Ephraim?"

"Are you alright, Rabbi? I heard you talking." A nurse stood beside him, a flashlight trained on his face. The golden haze continued to light up the room.

"I'm ok," Ephraim said. "Just discussing important matters with my friends."

The nurse inserted a digital thermometer into his ear. She pressed the call button.

"Can I help you?" the loudspeaker responded.

"It's Cindy. I'm in the burn unit. I need the resident."

Ephraim turned back to Elijah.

"The first Ephraim," Elijah continued, "followed the Almighty's directives completely. He behaved with humility and modesty. He was industrious and compassionate. His behaviour, his good works, and his passion for the Almighty attracted many others who eagerly joined the tribe, gave up their pagan ways, and swore loyalty to the One. His tribe grew in size and wealth. So did the other tribes of Israel. So numerous did they become and so rich, that Pharaoh came to fear them. You know the rest of the sad tale. Soon, the children of Israel found themselves enslaved."

"So, despite Ephraim's devotion to God, he ended up a slave," Alex commented.

Elijah shook his head. "No, this Ephraim brought only good to his tribe, as did the Ephraim who succeeded him. But the next Ephraim was rebellious, headstrong, immodest and dilatory in his observance of the Almighty's commandments."

"Hi, Rabbi Zimmerman, I'm Dr. Saunders. The nurse tells me you're running a high fever."

A young woman stood beside his bed, a bright, cheerful, bespectacled face framed by a mop of curly hair. She adjusted her stethoscope and listened carefully to his chest.

"Please don't disturb me," Ephraim said. "My friends and I are having a very serious discussion. I have a critical decision to make and I need their input."

"He's delirious," Ephraim heard the doctor say to the nurse. "Add an antibiotic to the drip line and check him every half-hour."

The nurse returned a moment later, hung a small bag on the pole behind him and connected it to the IV. Ephraim waited until she left.

"What happened to the third Ephraim?" he asked Elijah.

Again, he was not aware of leaving the hospital but found himself just inside a huge walled compound. From the glow of hundreds of campfires, he could make out scores of tents dotting the open space. The stench of rotting sewage fouled the air. As his eyes grew accustomed to the gloom, he could make out people sitting around the fires, talking, eating. Here and there a child cried, interrupting the low buzz of conversation. Overhead, stars filled the southern sky. A full moon eased above the horizon, its reflected light casting long shadows in the compound.

"Where the hell are we?" Alex asked.

"We are outside Pthom, one of the treasure cities the enslaved Israelites are building," Elijah explained. "Come, let us observe Ephraim."

He led them through the camp to its very centre. In front of a large tent, a cooking fire burned, heating a blackened bowl filled with a liquid that smelled of broth. Five men, all in long cloaks and barefoot, sat around the fire. They tore off chunks of flat bread and dipped them into the liquid. They ate in silence. Firelight glinted off sweaty, sun baked faces.

"Ephraim," a man with his back to the three observers said, "as usual, you do not listen to advice. Your plan is foolish and will not succeed."

The man opposite him spat into the fire, pulled back his headdress and stretched out his legs. He reminded Ephraim of Uncle Avram — tall, gaunt, with the long Zimmerman face. Only his dark beard ended the comparison. He leaned forward, speaking heatedly, bitterly.

"Aaron, did you enjoy your meal tonight? Was it not a sumptuous and just reward for the heavy work we did today? Are you happy living under the Egyptian yoke? In the days of Joseph, we had herds of cattle, flocks of chicken and other fowl, green pastures and lacked for nothing. Consider us now — slaves, impoverished, dying under the steady tyranny of our masters. The Almighty has forsaken us. You may wish to stay here waiting for your God to rescue you but I shall take the able men of my tribe and escape."

There were grunts of approval from the others.

"Where will you go?" Aaron objected. "If you leave here, you must leave Egypt. The army will pursue you."

Ephraim nodded. "Yes, the army will pursue, but we will have a head start. Tomorrow is our rest day this moon. We will be allowed out of the compound to wash by the river and to repair our tools. Tomorrow also starts a holy week for the Egyptians. They will be too busy with their festivities to force us back early into the compound. As for other of their holy days, only a small guard will be watching us. As soon as night falls, we will overcome the guard, take what weapons they have. The rest of us are armed with our staffs and tools."

"How many will you be?" Aaron asked.

"Twenty thousand, perhaps as many as thirty thousand. We will go to the promised land of Canaan."

Aaron shook his head so forcefully that his cloak fell down around his shoulders, revealing a full head of unkempt hair descending to a large beard. "Ephraim, God has spoken. He will take us away from here and into the land of Canaan. But we must wait until He signals we are ready. I have calculated that we can muster some six hundred thousand fighting men if we go as a united body. The Almighty's promise will be fulfilled, but we must wait for Him."

Ephraim laughed and spat. "And when will that be? Must we all die before your Almighty remembers us?"

"Ephraim," Aaron pleaded, "be not so wilful and contemptuous of the Almighty. It is blasphemy to speak as you do. Our time is coming. I can reveal to you now that I have met secretly with a Prince of Egypt who feels sympathy for us as a people and bemoans our plight. He has promised to help us. The Lord has whispered to me that this Prince is sincere and is the key to our salvation. We must wait."

Ephraim laughed again and spat even harder. "You are a fool, Aaron, to believe an Egyptian, let alone a Prince. He is dragging you along, ensuring you stay subservient, that we remain slaves. Nay, Aaron, argument is useless. Tomorrow night we are gone."

Aaron stood up and stretched supplicating arms to Ephraim. "I beg you, be not so impatient. Let me talk to the Prince who wants to help us so that you may confer with him. He will persuade you that the time of exodus is not yet upon us. Through him, the Almighty is preparing for the most auspicious moment. Our masters are powerful and not easily subdued. The enemies we will face in Canaan are also strong. We need the Almighty's help — we cannot overcome alone."

Ephraim stood up, towering over Aaron. "Am I a fool that I would reveal to a Prince of Egypt that I plan to depart? Even if he allowed me to live and tried to dissuade me, how would I know his advice is in our interest and not Egypt's? Who is this Prince that you have such confidence in him?"

Aaron looked around. The nearest campfire was some distance away. Nevertheless, he sat down and motioned the others to come closer. They formed a tight circle, their heads almost touching.

"I believe he is one of us," Aaron whispered. "There is a legend in our family that when the edict went out to kill all our newly first born male children, he was not seven days old. He would have been a victim except he was placed in a basket and hidden in a stream amidst the reeds and rushes. He was not discovered, so the story goes, until Pharaoh's daughter came to the stream to wash and heard him whimpering. She took him to the palace and brought him up as an Egyptian. I was a few years older and knew nothing of this. Only recently did my sister Miriam tell me the story. This Prince of Egypt is my brother."

There was a moment's silence. Then Ephraim and the other three broke out into raucous laughter until the tears streamed down their faces.

"A wonderful story, Aaron," Ephraim chortled. "Nevertheless, we leave tomorrow. I go now to my tent to enjoy one more night with my favourite wife. It will be many moons before we see each other again."

Ephraim disappeared into the tent. The other three also left. Aaron, head bowed, hands clasped behind his back, walked slowly away.

A beeping sound in his ear brought Ephraim back to his hospital bed.

"Your fever's come down slightly,' the nurse said.

"Did Ephraim actually take off?" Alex asked. "I never knew that some of the Israelites left early."

"It's an old legend," Ephraim answered.

"Your fever is no legend," the nurse insisted. "But don't worry. The antibiotic will soon fix it."

"What happened?" Alex asked. "Did the tribe make it?"

"It's a tragic story," Ephraim said.

"Fever is serious but hardly a tragedy," the nurse said reassuringly.

Ephraim looked at the nurse. "It's got nothing to do with fever. The premature departure of Ephraim and the able-bodied men of the tribe was a tragedy."

The nurse raised her eyebrows. "I think, Rabbi, we're not on the same page. Let me cool your face."

She washed his face with a towel dipped in cold water and then left.

"Come, my sons," Elijah commanded. "Let us discover what happens when the directives of the Almighty are not followed."

They were standing beside the Nile, not far from the walled compound. Further upriver, Ephraim saw the soaring stelae, obelisks and massive buildings of Pthom. A red sun was just dipping below the western horizon, lighting up a few fluffy clouds in a clear darkening sky. The Nile flowed quickly past, its waters slopping over its banks. It must be springtime, Ephraim thought, the Nile is in flood. The land, green and luxuriant, climbed slowly upwards, past the compound and to the sandy coloured hills, standing out against the crimson sunset.

A man came out of the compound and walked hurriedly towards the river and followed it downstream.

"Hey, there goes Aaron," Alex exclaimed. "Finally, a biblical hero my height."

"Let us accompany him," Elijah said.

They overtook Aaron but kept a few feet behind him. Despite his short legs, Aaron strode rapidly along until he came to a narrow stream that emptied into the Nile. He leapt across the stream, turned up to a small copse of alder bushes flanking the stream, and disappeared into their shelter.

Within the copse, there was still enough light to make out Aaron and other men, some standing, some lying in the shadows. A tall gaunt man, face blistered and scarred with festering gashes, fell on his knees and clasped Aaron.

"Aaron, is it indeed you? Forgive me, I beg of you and the Almighty. I have sinned grievously."

Aaron looked around and pushed Ephraim back. "Ephraim, what has happened to you? Where are the others?"

Ephraim shook his head. "There are no others. We are but ten. The Almighty has exacted retribution on us. I wish He had spared the others and taken me instead."

Aaron grasped Ephraim by the shoulders.

"What are you saying? Where are all the fighters you left with?"

Ephraim pulled free from Aaron and sat down on the ground, his head bowed. The cowl of his cloak had fallen off his head and his face glistened with tears.

"All gone, either dead or enslaved. The Philistines met us at Gath. There were too many of them. We fought bravely but were overcome. My brave men lie unburied in the fields of Gath, their bones bleaching in the sun. We alone managed to escape. We are all that is left."

Some of the others crowded around him. One of them, a haggard looking man in a torn cloak, leaning on a staff touched him reassuringly on a shoulder. "Despair not, Ephraim. You are a great leader and did your best. The Almighty forsook us."

"Nay," Aaron responded, contempt and anger hardening his voice, "you forsook the Almighty. Our great father Jacob saw promise in you. What would he think now?"

Ephraim prostrated himself before Aaron. "You are right to be harsh with us, Aaron, but I promise you we will rebuild. We seek no more adventures. We accept that your guidance comes from the Almighty and we will adhere to it. Henceforth, you may have confidence that we will be loyal to you and to all the tribes of Israel."

Aaron sighed and was silent for a moment. "Stand up, Ephraim, we will return to the compound. There, food and drink await you."

Ephraim looked at Aaron suspiciously. "Will the guards not stop us? I wonder, too, how did you know we were hiding here?"

"The Prince I told you about knows you are here and informed me. Just as I was able to leave the compound, so you will pass into it unscathed."

Ephraim peered uneasily through the bushes to the darkening fields. "How do we know this is not a trap?"

"Ephraim, once again you are foolish. If the Prince wanted to kill you or capture you, he had ample opportunity to do so. He is dedicated to helping us. It is God's will. You have promised loyalty. Put aside your rebellious nature and trust in the Almighty."

"You are right, Aaron," Ephraim said.

He motioned to his men and all followed Aaron out of the copse and towards the compound. Some of them limped; others leaned heavily on their staffs. Two clasped arms around a third and helped him along. All their robes and cloaks were torn and ragged.

Elijah, Alex and Ephraim watched them go until they disappeared into the night.

CHAPTER 12

The Woman Of Nahel Sorek

It was dark now. Elijah led Ephraim and Alex back to the Nile and they sat close to its bank. The splashing, rippling water had a calming effect and generated a sense of tranquillity, despite the tragic results they had observed of Ephraim's foray into Canaan.

"Our Lord can be terrible in his anger," Ephraim said.

"The Almighty demands loyalty. It is an essential part of the Covenant," insisted Elijah. "Ephraim's rebelliousness cost him dearly."

"I just don't agree," Alex objected. "It had nothing to do with God. Aaron's strategy was right on. Six hundred thousand men acting as a united front and waiting for the right moment was better than twenty to thirty thousand men rushing off without even a plan. What do you expect? They met a larger army, probably better armed and on its own turf."

"Nay, my son, had the Almighty favoured them, they would have succeeded, just as David — a puny boy — was able to subdue the giant Goliath."

Alex shrugged his shoulders. "I don't agree with that either. David knew he couldn't go up against Goliath with sword and buckler, so he used a weapon he was familiar with and which kept him out of the giant's reach. It was David's cunning and skill that won him the day. Afterwards, everyone claimed that God must have been on his side."

Ephraim half-listened to the ongoing argument between Elijah and Alex. Their positions were quite clear. Elijah believed that all events were God-driven. Alex insisted that events were either natural or caused by human agency, and affected by chance. For Ephraim, this was no specious debate. He was profoundly disturbed by the scenes he had witnessed. They supported

Elijah's view that unquestioning loyalty to God was paramount and deviation could be catastrophic. He had his own personal experience as evidence.

Yet he loved Laura fervently. Much of his memory regarding her and their relationship had come back. She wasn't as beautiful as Rebecca but still very attractive. He had enjoyed her body, cupping her breasts with his large hands, the feel of her round buttocks and shapely thighs. Were his feelings totally physical? He thought not — he liked her humour, her down-to-earth manner, and her honesty. He was also impressed how quickly she had decided to change her religion in order to support him in his.

As for Rebecca, his mother was quite right. In terms of someone who could integrate with him as a rabbi and teacher, Rebecca was the better choice. He could see himself learning to love her. After all, she was very beautiful, dynamic and determined. He relished her extreme religiosity even though he found it cramping at times.

His mind swung back and forth between the two women, deciding at one moment to accept Rebecca, then torn back to Laura. The conflict within him became a frenzy of uncertainty and doubt, terror and despair. He began to sweat profusely.

He swung around and immersed his legs in the Nile, sighing with relief as cool refreshing water lapped his knees. He plunged both arms into the river up to his elbows.

"Sorry, Rabbi, but this will lower your temperature," a soft female voice said. "Your fever is just too high."

Ephraim opened his eyes. Two nurses were applying towels dipped in ice cold water to his arms and legs. The golden haze lit up the far side of the room where Elijah and Alex facing each other continued to argue. A morning sun sliced through the parallel slats of the window blinds and patterned the floor with black and white stripes.

"I prefer the Nile," Ephraim said. "I wish you'd left me there."

"As soon as you get better, you can go back to the Nile," a nurse said as she massaged his face with a wet washcloth.

Elijah walked over. "There is no need to return to the Nile. The Israelites have long departed."

Ephraim held out a supplicating hand. "But the Nile was so cool, so refreshing. I have a terribly difficult decision to make. The Nile gave me the serenity I need to think clearly. Please, Eliyahu, take me back." Ephraim tried to sit up.

A nurse gently restrained him. "No, Rabbi, you must be calm. We must get your fever down otherwise you may start convulsing."

Alex sat on the bed opposite and called out, "Freml, the decision is not difficult. Stop fretting. You break no laws when you marry Laura."

"Pay no attention to him, my son," Elijah countered. "The Almighty speaks through me and forbids wedding the Midianite."

Ephraim wrested his arms from the nurses and grasped his head. "I need some time to think."

The nurses pulled his arms back gently and continued their ministrations. "Relax and take all the time you want," one of the nurses said.

Ephraim closed his eyes and slept.

He sat at the river's edge, his arms and legs immersed in the flowing current. A brilliant moon lit up the night and glinted on the water. The plashing of the river was the only sound in the otherwise pervasive silence. Despite his internal turmoil, he experienced again a long moment of tranquillity and peace. It's so nice to be alone, he thought, and to work through my dilemma on my own, no advice, and no argument, just me, laying out the options, alternatives, and then deciding the best course to take.

He heard a faint rhythmic splashing in the river. A shadow moved across the water which soon became an open boat propelled by oarsmen, gliding towards him. Its prow touched the bank and a lithe figure stepped down and sat beside him.

"Ephraim, sweetheart, can you hear me? I love you so much. I'm so eager to have you better." Laura leaned over and kissed him. "Everybody wants you better. My mother prays for you in church and I go to the synagogue and pray. Even Polly — who has her own grief — calls every day to see how you're doing."

Ephraim put an arm around her and they clasped each other.

"Tell Polly, Alex is fine. We talk quite often now."

"You talk to Alex? But Alex is …" Laura stopped short and began to weep.

"Don't take him too seriously, Miss," said a female voice which seemed to come from the boat. "He's delirious. As soon as the fever breaks, he'll be back to normal."

Laura kissed him again. "Please get better. I need you so badly. We have so much to talk about — my studies, for example — there are questions that only you can help me with."

Ephraim stroked her arm and said reassuringly, "You mustn't worry. It's so pleasant and cool by the river, that I feel better already."

"By the river? What river?" Laura asked.

"The river Nile. The river your boat is on."

A male voice from the boat called out: "Time to go, Miss."

Laura kissed Ephraim again. He felt the tears on her face and tasted their saltiness. He grasped her hand and held her back. "You mustn't cry. Come back soon."

Laura stepped carefully into the boat. The oarsmen back-oared and the boat gently pulled away and swept downstream.

His desire to be alone was short-lived. Two shadows came into view walking along the river bank and slowly approached him.

"Freml, darling, it's your mother," one of them whispered into his ear.

"Ma," Ephraim responded happily. "What a nice surprise. How did you find me?"

"Where else could you be, my Freml? You've been here a long time."

Ephraim shook his head. "No, ma, I haven't been here very long. I'd love to stay here. The Nile is so peaceful and serene, especially at night."

"He's delirious, Mrs. Zimmerman. He imagines he's somewhere else," a vaguely familiar female voice said softly.

Ephraim peered intently at the other shadow but the face was shrouded in darkness. Then the moon came out from behind a fleeting cloud.

"Rebecca!" he exclaimed. "How nice to see you. I've been discussing my future with a couple of friends and your name comes up as one of my options."

"How very interesting," Rebecca said. "After the harsh words we had before your accident, I suppose I should be grateful that I'm at least an option. An option for what?"

Ephraim heard the stiffness in her voice and realized he was on sensitive ground. Better not tell her that Laura is the other option. "You remember the debates we had whether the Bible was literally true or metaphor. Well, I know now that the Egyptian enslavement was no metaphor and that Moses and Aaron really existed. I saw it with my own eyes."

"Freml, oy my Freml," Marsha whispered sadly. "What is happening with you?"

Rebecca rubbed his shoulder affectionately and kissed him on the cheek. "Ephraim, forget about our debates. Just get better. I'm making great progress with my school. I need your help. There's a job waiting for you."

"Listen to what she says, Freml," Marsha said, gently stroking his face.

Ephraim began to shiver as the cold river water penetrated through him. Marsha called the nurse. Twin beeps in his ear snapped him back to his hospital bed.

"Hi, Rabbi, it's me, Cindy, your nurse. Your fever's down quite a bit and I'm removing the ice packs."

Ephraim was quite awake now but closed his eyes and pretended to sleep. He so much wanted to be alone. He found the presence of the two women vaguely disturbing. They reminded him that he was wrestling with a decision — Rebecca versus Laura. He favoured Laura. It was only Elijah's spirited opposition, reinforced by the biblical scenes he had witnessed, that had caused him to reconsider. Alex's views were equally compelling but Alex did not believe in a personal God that intervened in human affairs.

Although he had doubts from time to time, Ephraim accepted that a personal God existed and must be honoured, prayed to, propitiated, and, above all, obeyed. He believed that he and Laura had addressed all the concerns that the orthodox community might have but Elijah disagreed.

"You are quite right," Elijah said. "I do not agree."

Ephraim opened his eyes. His mother and Rebecca were gone and the nurse was nowhere in sight. The golden haze had returned and outshone the sunlight streaming through the window. Elijah stood on one side of his bed, Alex on the other.

"Why do you object?" Alex asked. "Laura will be Jewish before they marry. Lots of biblical heroes did not marry Israelites. You're being too harsh on my friend."

Elijah did not look at Alex but stared hard at Ephraim. "Your point is well taken, my errant son. Our forefathers and leaders were unswerving in their faith. There was no danger that the women they wed could sway them. But Ephraim's faith falls short of the strength required. He has confessed to having doubts. To placate his woman, he is prepared to allow other gods into his household."

"Freml, what's he talking about?"

Ephraim sighed. "I once told Laura that if Jesus was that important to her, she could continue to pray to him. But that was before she decided to become Jewish. Since she started her studies, she's never mentioned it again."

"That's it, Elijah. Your objections are overruled. Case closed." Alex mimicked banging a gavel.

"Nay, my son, be not too hasty to dismiss my prophesies. Ephraim's carnal desire for the Midianite will usurp his reason and faith. I see it clearly — he will be led away from the full observance of God's commandments."

"There you have it, Freml," Alex said mockingly. "The next time you see Laura, don't say, 'I love you' say, 'I carnal desire you' or if she asks 'what do you want for dinner' say 'carnal desire, lots of it and well done.' Freml, your Elijah's from a bygone era. You've done everything you're supposed to do. Send him packing."

Despite Alex's impudence, Ephraim couldn't help smiling.

"Your friend is not amusing." Elijah was clearly irritated. He gathered his cloak around him tightly and looked at both of them grimly. "These are not frivolous matters. My prophecies are not to be disregarded. What you do will have consequences well beyond your power to predict. Our sacred history is replete with those who followed the Almighty and were rewarded and those who did not and were punished. Even Moses was not allowed into Canaan because of a minor infraction. After Ephraim's rebellious moment and its tragic outcome, he excelled in his devotion to the Lord and the tribe prospered. His successor, Joshua, also completely observant of the Almighty's commandments and directives, led the Israelites into Canaan, defeated the foes who opposed them, and settled the tribes in their allotted territories. As long as the tribe Ephraim remained steadfast in its Godliness, it continued to prosper and grow. When it became idolatrous and uncaring about the word of God, it was conquered by Assyria and dispersed like chaff thrown into the wind."

"But, Eliyahu," Alex argued, 'your point is always the same. If a battle is won, they were good people and God was on their side — if a battle is lost, they must have been bad because God withdrew his support. Your examples don't bear on Ephraim's case. He's not leading armies into battle. All he wants is to marry the girl he loves."

EPHRAIM

"As earlier I spoke, I object to the Midianite because she will lead him astray and his faith is not strong enough to resist. If the scenes we have witnessed are not sufficient to convince you, come, let us observe an example that will illustrate my concern."

They stood beside a wide stream in a narrow valley with hills on either side. A hot sun rode high in a cloudless sky. While the hills looked parched, the valley was verdant with tall green grass and the occasional grove of date palms. In the distance they could see a small village.

"Let us follow the waterway," Elijah directed.

After the confinement of his hospital bed, Ephraim felt liberated as he surveyed the bucolic countryside and the stream curving lazily across the meadows. Now and then, they saw herds of sheep grazing the thick grass, watched over by wary shepherds. Here and there, the land fell and the stream cascaded down and continued on its way. There were fences of brambles surrounding patches of cultivation. At one point, a line of willow flanked the stream. They stepped around a dozing shepherd and his flock sheltering under the trees from the hot sun.

They reached a village consisting of a score of mud-brick houses with thatched roofs, clustered close to the stream. The midday sun appeared to have driven most of the villagers into their houses, except for a few women and some men who sat in the shade of a palm grove, talking quietly and eating. One house was larger than the others and was set well back. A woman emerged from the house, carrying a large urn, and walked towards the well they were standing around.

"Wow!" Alex exclaimed. "There's one hot babe."

She was indeed beautiful, Ephraim thought. She wore a long white gown, clasped at the waist by a narrow bronze circlet which emphasized her voluptuous figure. Light olive skin enhanced the even features of her face, aquiline nose and dark eyes. Her brown hair flowed freely past her shoulders midway to her waist. Her feet were bare. To avoid dragging her gown through the wet around the well, she lifted the skirt to reveal shapely ankles and calves.

She put down the urn, and still holding her skirt, lowered a wooden bucket into the well. She had difficulty pulling up the filled bucket.

"Woman of Nahal Sorek, may I help you?"

They looked towards the owner of the voice. A giant of a man stood on the other side of the stream. He must be seven-feet tall, Ephraim marvelled. The man was broad in the shoulder with powerful muscular arms, torso and legs. He was bare down to the sheepskin skirt secured to his waist by a leather thong. A short iron sword was thrust into the thong. His feet were encased in thick leather sandals laced to his knees.

A square face rounded by a full beard, and framed by long braided hair, featured, under bushy brows, blue eyes that darted suspiciously around. He held a staff the thickness of a young tree topped by a large round boll. Despite his size, he spoke in a pleasantly soft voice that resonated across the stream.

For a moment, the woman seemed repelled by the offer and shrank back. Then she recovered herself and smiled. "Of course, you may. This is heavy work for a weak woman."

Ephraim noticed the villagers under the palm trees quickly dispersed and ran to their dwellings.

The stream was ten feet wide at this point, but the man leapt it easily. He pulled up the water bucket with one hand and poured it carefully into the urn.

"Let me carry it for you," he said.

She did not object and led the way towards her house.

"What is your name?" he asked.

She looked at him coquettishly. "It is not proper for a woman to give her name to a stranger. You must first tell me who you are, where you are from, and where you are going."

"You know who I am, woman of Nahal Sorek, and where I am from. Where I go is where my enemies are."

She stopped and turned to face him. "I am not your enemy, Lord Samson of Israel, nor does this village pose any threat to you. I am grateful for your help but you need not stop here."

Samson smiled. "You need have no fear. I was merely passing on my way to Gaza when I saw your fair face and form. I wish to make your acquaintance."

They continued walking. "My name is Delilah. I live in the house of my father who has long since departed this world. I knew not my mother for she died at my birth."

By now, they had reached her house. A maidservant took the urn from Samson and waited for her mistress.

"Thank you, Lord Samson," Delilah said bowing. "My servant will help me now."

"It is hot and the coolness of your house will refresh me." It seemed more like a command than a suggestion.

A worried frown puckered her forehead, but Delilah stood her ground: "It is not meet for a woman to invite a man into her dwelling where she lives alone. Perhaps if you return just before sunset, you may share my evening meal with me in the garden."

"I shall take shelter in yon grove and wait out the day impatiently." Samson trudged off, stamping his staff in irritation.

"We will wait here," Elijah said to Ephraim and Alex.

The three sat down on the soft grass.

"It's a long wait," Ephraim said, leaning back on his elbows.

Alex stretched out on the ground. "Maybe Elijah will fast forward the action."

The time did go by quickly and the sun was soon poised above the horizon. Samson stood before the door and hit it twice with the boll of his staff. The sound reverberated throughout the village but no one appeared. The houses seemed devoid of people.

A maidservant led Samson around the house and through a gate on the east side. The garden ran the length of the house and was protected by a waist high stone fence. In the centre was a small pond bordered by large flat stones. Beside the pond, there were two stuffed pillows separated by a low table. The maidservant motioned him to remove his sandals and then washed his feet. Delilah came out of the house, dressed in a beige linen cloak tied at the waist with a linen belt encrusted with glass beads.

She bowed. "Welcome, Lord Samson. Please sit down." She motioned to the far pillow. He waited until she was seated. She called out and two maidservants appeared carrying platters of food and two goblets which they set on the low table. They returned, one carrying a ceramic pot which she placed on a flat stone next to the table, the other held a bulging gourd and prepared to pour it into the goblet in front of Samson.

Samson placed his hand over the goblet. "If that is wine, I may not drink it. Cool water is all I wish."

"But, Lord Samson," Delilah objected, looking hurt, "this is excellent wine from the fields of Ashkelon. Surely you will do me the honour of tasting it."

"I do not doubt it is very good," Samson said. "My God forbids me to drink wine."

"Then ignore your god and worship mine," Delilah countered. "Dagon does not deny us this pleasure."

Samson grimaced. "There is only one God and He is mine. I will not drink the wine."

Delilah turned to the maidservant. "Our guest prefers water."

They helped themselves to the platters. There were hard-boiled eggs swimming in salt water, crushed walnuts mixed with honey, minced chick peas laced with olive oil, boiled lima beans seasoned with lemon zest, and olives.

"You must try the stew," Delilah said, pulling the ceramic pot towards her. "It has simmered many hours. I know your people do not eat boar which is our favourite, therefore I have substituted lamb." She ladled out steaming chunks of lamb, fragrant with sesame, cumin, cinnamon and onion onto wooden plates. They scooped up the stew with flatbread, and finished off the meal with wedges of melon. Delilah exclaimed in delight as Samson tore into the food.

"Delilah of Nahal Sorek, you have neither father nor husband. How do you live?"

Delilah hesitated a moment. "I do what women in my situation must do. I have many suitors."

Samson laughed. "Suitors or paying guests? It matters not. I have desire for you. I will be your suitor — your only suitor."

Delilah smiled demurely. "I must be persuaded. My suitors are very generous."

Samson swept aside the table, platters and food remnants and picked Delilah up from her cushion. He pulled apart her cloak and tore the white tunic underneath, revealing her very full breasts. He kissed her wildly, starting at the top of her head and working down to the breasts. Delilah moaned, her head fell back, and her mouth slackened with lust.

"Wow!" Alex said. "This is better than the Blue Movie Channel."

"Not here," Delilah whispered. "Carry me into the house."

They followed Samson and Delilah.

Just inside the house was a large room. A thick mattress, covered in linen spreads and pillows, occupied one corner. A chest of drawers made from palm wood stood against the wall. Opposite the bed, two large wooden divan chairs, luxuriously appointed with stuffed linen sheets were arranged parallel to each other with a low table in between.

Elijah and Ephraim stood but Alex stretched out on one of the divan chairs.

"Oh, what I wouldn't give for a video cam," Alex said.

Samson stood Delilah beside the bed, pulled off her cloak and ripped the remainder of her tunic. She threw her arms around him and nestled her body against his full erection.

Despite his strength and passion, he gently laid her on the bed and mounted her. As the orgasm took her, she screamed and bit into his shoulder. He continued to kiss her and then withdrew and rolled over on his back, his penis flaccid and slick.

Delilah snuggled up against him and put an arm across his chest. "Lord Samson, you may be my only suitor. I want no others."

He ran his fingers through her hair. "I will reside here for a time and then I will take you to my father's house in Zorah. There we will wed."

They made love many more times that night and then fell asleep in each others arms. They awoke when the sun was high.

For the three observers, the night had shot by quickly. They followed the two lovers into the garden.

"Lord Samson," Delilah asked hesitantly while they, swathed in linen sheets, breakfasted in the garden, "when we wed, must I swear loyalty to your god and forswear my own?"

"Of course," Samson replied firmly. "I am a Judge of Israel. My household must set an example for all Israelites."

Delilah sat on his lap and put her arms around his neck. The linen sheet fell down, exposing her breasts. "But, sweet Samson, Dagon is my god and has helped me through many difficult times. Surely, if I am discreet and not open about my worship, I may continue to pray to Dagon."

"Dagon is a false god and cannot be tolerated in my household," Samson replied gruffly.

Delilah removed her arms from around his neck, pouted, but remained on his lap.

"Then I cannot wed you. You may kill me if you wish." Arms akimbo, she raised her head haughtily, a look of determination on her face.

Samson was distraught. "Why are you so stubborn. The God of Israel is a more powerful god than your Dagon, and as my wife, will grant you special favours. You will lose these privileges if you worship Dagon."

"And you will lose the pleasurable privileges of my body." She wiggled her buttocks against his thighs and felt his immediate response. She stood up and walked away, the linen sheet falling to the ground.

"Woman, you drive me wild." He strode after her but she turned and faced him. She spat out her words contemptuously. "The Judge of Israel has killed many soldiers of Philistija. Does he also rape their women?"

Samson paused. His desire subsided. "Samson does not rape."

They resumed their seats opposite each other and finished in silence their breakfast of melons, dates and figs. There was a coolness between them now.

Delilah began to weep. "Why are *you* so stubborn?" she said between sobs. "You profess desire for me and declare we will wed but you will not grant me a simple request that will cost you nothing. You are asking me to leave my people and live among yours but I cannot even take my god with me, a memento to help me feel at home. I need not have asked permission of you. I could have prayed to Dagon secretly. But I chose to be honest with my husband, to keep nothing from him, and my reward is disappointment and despair."

"What you ask for may cost me dearly," a troubled Samson said. "It may remove the favour my God bestows upon me."

"Is your god so jealous that your woman's secret observance of Dagon will upset him? Will he take away your strength?"

"I do not believe so. I will not worship Dagon but will continue to obey the one true God and to follow the other conditions that my God has imposed in order for me to maintain my strength."

"Then I will bring my Dagon with me. Not even you will know when I pray to him."

Samson frowned and looked worried. "It still troubles me, allowing Dagon into my father's house."

"Then let me resolve your qualms." She pushed him off the pillow and down onto the grass and straddled his thighs. He went quickly erect and she eased him into her. It was too much for him. He sat up, grasped her tightly, and rocked back and forth until the orgasm came.

"I can deny you nothing," he said after they had dressed and were standing in the bedroom facing each other and holding hands. "I desire you too much. I love you."

She looked up at him fondly. "And I love you and will be a true and faithful wife. I will learn to worship your god even as I harbour mine. I will not shame you."

Elijah grasped Ephraim and Alex each by a shoulder. "Behold this scene. Thus did the decline of Samson, Judge of Israel, begin."

"I don't know about decline," Alex said. "For a middle-aged guy, he sure could screw. I counted five times during the night and once now."

Elijah humphed disgustedly, but Ephraim smiled affectionately at his friend. "Alex, you're missing the point. It shows how smitten Samson was by Delilah as I was by Laura. Samson, at least, was uneasy about allowing Dagon into his house. I wasn't even troubled when I agreed that Laura could bring her Jesus."

"No, no, no, Freml, don't start wallowing in guilt and self-recrimination. That's what your prophet wants. Did Delilah really love Samson — she eventually betrays him. But Laura loves you, really, really, loves you. You said that she has never mentioned Jesus, once she started her Jewish studies. The two cases are not at all the same."

"I do not make comparisons between the Philistine and the Midianite," Elijah noted sternly. "I merely observe that in the throes of carnal desire, some men are prepared to compromise their devotion to the Almighty. Samson is an example of the tragic consequences that follow."

He turned to face Ephraim. "In your case, the Israelite woman is stronger in our faith than you are. She will never tempt you to diverge from your dedication to God."

"Eliyahu, you *are* making comparisons," Alex objected. "You're presuming the Midianite will not become as strong as the Israelite. How can you be so certain?"

Elijah drew himself up to his full height, gathered his cloak tightly around him and looked sadly at Alex. "I am a prophet. I know."

"Weather forecasters are also prophets," Alex snapped. "They…"

"Alex," Ephraim interrupted, "you're going too far. You don't have to agree with Eliyahu but at least be respectful."

"OK, I'm sorry, I'll be more respectful. All I was getting at was Eliyahu's example does not apply to you. You're not a Samson, and Laura — sure, she's pretty — is not a Delilah. Did God really cause Delilah to betray Samson because he gave in on Dagon? I think she would've betrayed him anyway. Besides, why did she betray him? Was it patriotism?"

"I don't think so," Ephraim replied. "The Philistines offered her 1100 pieces of silver to discover the secret of Samson's strength."

"1100 pieces of silver!" Alex exclaimed. "Delilah was a much better negotiator than Judas. Freml, Laura will be true to you even if the entire Church comes down on her. Let's face it. It was Samson's choice of woman that got him into trouble. If he'd stayed close to home and married a local girl, he'd've been ok."

"That is just my point," thundered Elijah, "and the essence of my prophecy."

Alex looked sheepish. "I guess I blundered into that one."

"It's ok, Alex. I know what you're trying to say. All this argument has left me in a real quandary. If I were more like you, I would've married Laura by now. Even now I ache to see her. But I'm a Rabbi. I can't ignore Elijah's advice. I have to take it into consideration. I have to decide whether whom I marry will please or offend my God. I've got to really think this through, and it would be best if I went back to my hospital bed."

CHAPTER 13

Decisions, Decisions

"You're in your hospital bed."

Ephraim opened his eyes, wincing at the bright morning sun lighting up the room. Cindy, the nurse, was looking down on him, a worried frown on her face.

"You've been talking in your sleep again. How do you feel? Your fever's gone."

"I'm feeling fine, nice and cool. A lot better than the other day."

"At the height of your fever, you insisted you were at the Nile. Have you been anywhere since?" Cindy smiled solicitously at him.

"Well, if you really want to know I was at Nahal Sorek, the Brook of Sorek."

Cindy manipulated the bed until he was in a sitting position. She placed a bowl of water, a washcloth and toiletry articles on his lap.

"Wash yourself and brush your teeth. Funny, your dreams seem to centre on water. I wonder if it has something to do with the burns you received."

He shrugged his shoulders, and gingerly washed his face, still sensitive to the burns that were now scarred over. Cindy returned, accompanied by an orderly. They helped him off the bed and into a chair beside his bed.

"If you feel well enough, you have some early morning visitors."

Although he was feeling giddy and exhausted and had looked forward to being alone, he nodded and leaned back in his chair. His first visitor was Irving, who stood awkwardly at the foot of his bed.

"Hi, Freml, how ya doing?"

"Sort of ok."

Irving came a step closer. "I hear you've been feverish and delirious."

Ephraim nodded. "That's probably why I feel so worn out. I've been all over ancient Egypt and Israel."

Irving looked at him oddly. "These were dreams?"

"Who knows? They may have been but as far as I'm concerned, I was there."

Irving shifted his feet uneasily. "Well, anyway, where are you now?"

Ephraim smiled. "My favourite spot — Sacred Grace. Even a rabbi pays homage to this great Catholic teaching hospital."

Irving laughed. "Freml, I've got my father-in-law and Gertie waiting in the visitors lounge. They'd like to say hello but after what happened the last time they were here, they wanted me to test the waters first. Between you and me, I told my father-in-law he was a real shmock — well, I didn't exactly say it like that but he got the message. He's really sorry. Will you see them?"

"What a question, Irving. They're close family. Of course, they can come in."

"You sure? I told Avram 'no arguing.'"

Ephraim nodded. Uncle Avram, a welcoming smile on his face, shook Ephraim's hand and Gertie kissed him on the forehead. Irving stayed back a few paces.

"You're looking a lot better, Freml, since we saw you last," Gertie said.

Uncle Avram nodded. "I hope they're treating you well," he said.

They made small talk for a while, and then there was a moment of silence. Uncle Avram cleared his throat and then began somewhat hesitantly, "Freml, I'd like to ask you a favour. I know I was stupid the way I told you about Alex and I apologize. Can you forgive me?"

Ephraim reached out and grasped Avram's hand. "Uncle Avram, there is nothing to forgive. I think I reacted the way I did because I knew in my heart of hearts that Alex was gone. After I awoke from the coma, nobody ever mentioned him and neither he nor Polly came to visit. I just couldn't handle having my worst fears confirmed."

Avram pumped his hand. "Freml, you have no idea how happy that makes me feel. Now, could you put in a good word for me to your mother? She hasn't talked to me since we were here last."

Old men also have love needs, Ephraim thought. "I'll tell her we've sorted things out. But, Uncle Avram, it's up to her."

"Of course, Freml, but a word from you will smooth things over. It's difficult to make your mother happy. Already, she was anxious when you, the only child, went off to New York. Then your father of blessed memory left us and she was inconsolable for a long time. Then you announce your marriage plans …"

"Papa, don't go there," Irving admonished.

Avram hesitated then carried on. "Well, you know Marsha wasn't happy about your marriage plans. But worst was the accident and the long time we weren't sure you'd make it. We have to make her happy again. I know how you can do it but Irving will stop me from saying it."

"Papa," said Irving, "you promised me 'no arguing.' Freml has to recover first and, in his own time, will decide for himself. He doesn't need anybody's advice."

Uncle Avram looked sternly at his son-in-law. "Irving, I'm not arguing. All I want to say is the girl is no good. She's already caused one death and Freml will be scarred for life."

Ephraim was becoming more distraught as Avram lectured him. He still felt somehow guilty for Alex's death and was reminded that he had never properly grieved for him. He bowed his head and could not stop the tears from flowing. He stood up unsteadily and intoned the Prayer for the Dead.

Irving threw up his hands in disgust and glared at his father-in-law. "Gertie, let's go."

Gertie said, "Papa, Freml needs rest."

Avram clearly wanted to continue his tirade but the two took him firmly by the arms and hustled him out of the room.

Ephraim finished the prayer and sat down heavily in the chair. Until the accident, he had been so certain. He liked Rebecca but loved Laura. She was doing everything she could to accommodate him and to fit in with Judaic law and traditions. Why then would God object to her? True, in his eagerness for Laura, he had made statements that could be construed as forsaking the strict conditions of his faith and calling. While their children would be raised in accordance with Jewish requirements, he'd have to contend with the influence of her family. Rebecca would present no such dangers. Elijah was right — Rebecca was more orthodox than he. The two women could help him in his work in different ways. Laura would never accuse him of secular thinking and would bring a sense of social justice and compassion, whereas Rebecca would be more traditional and biblical. He needed both. Elijah's initial advice was apt — wed them both.

When Cindy came in to check on him, Ephraim was still seated, head bowed, chin resting on chest.

"Rabbi, are you ok?"

He lifted his head, his cheeks still wet with tears.

"Were those three too much for you? Shall we just not let them in anymore?"

He shook his head.

"You'll be going into surgery shortly for another skin graft. Your mother and your girlfriend are here, waiting in the visitors lounge. They'd like to see you before you go and they'll be here when you return. There are two other women with them — a Miss Zifkin and your girlfriend's mother. Do you think you're up for a visit? You need some exercise. We could walk you over to the lounge."

He agreed even though he continued to feel giddy and weak. The orderly and Cindy helped him, and each supporting an arm, guided him carefully to the door and into the hallway. They held on to him tightly.

"You don't seem very steady," Cindy observed. "Shall we go back?"

He shook his head and continued his slow and awkward pace.

"The moment has arrived," the orderly said, but it was Elijah who walked beside him and held his arm. "Both the Israelite and the Midianite await you. You must shun the Midianite and choose the Israelite."

"Don't listen to him." Alex had replaced Cindy. "You want a happy life, then Laura's for you."

"For God's sake," Ephraim pleaded. "Leave me in peace."

"We can't," Cindy said. "I'm afraid you'll fall."

A wave of dizziness swept over Ephraim. Alex stood in front of him. "Freml, you've done nothing wrong. Don't change your mind. Marry Laura, the woman you truly love and who has sacrificed for you."

"Your friend wallows in cattle dung," Elijah shouted in his ear. "He is the evil eye, the tempter who seduces you from the true path. The Almighty speaks through me and the message is clear. Stray not as Samson did."

"Rabbi, you've stopped walking. Shall we go back?" Cindy asked.

"No, I want to see my visitors but my friends are blocking the way."

"OK, we're going back. You're getting delirious again."

"No, I must see them. I have a decision to make." Ephraim mustered his strength, and pushed Elijah and Alex aside, and dragged Cindy and the orderly along.

"Caution, my boy," thundered Elijah. "You will make the wrong decision if you listen to your friend and act impetuously. The very essence of your time in this world depends upon it."

"It's nonsense, Freml," countered Alex loudly. "Rebecca is not the essence of your life on this Earth, Laura is. Elijah's back in BC, we're in the 21st century. The rules have changed, even the orthodox rules."

Elijah was strident, angry, as he screamed at Ephraim, "I am the Prophet Elijah. Those who defy me end up tragically. I have advised you since childhood. You cannot forswear me now."

Alex was equally loud as he retorted, "Freml, I've been your friend and soul buddy since we were little boys. We've helped each other all the way through. If you listen to this guy, you'll screw up your life."

Ephraim reached the door of the visitors lounge. Sitting in easy chairs and facing each other were his mother and Rebecca on one side and Laura and her mother on the other.

All four smiled at him and stood up. He saw the look of love on Rebecca's face and the look of love on Laura's. He stared at each of them as they came towards him. Elijah was pointing at Rebecca; Alex was pointing at Laura. Ephraim felt another wave of dizziness come over him. Colour drained out of his face, and as he fell back into the arms of Cindy and the orderly, he screamed, "I don't know what to do."

CHAPTER 14

The Rabbi Decides

He felt himself picked up and eased into a wheelchair and rolled back to his bed. He heard Cindy advise his four visitors to wait in the lounge. He was prodded by a stethoscope and his arm clasped by a blood pressure cuff. Twin beeps in his ear signalled the thermometer.

He opened his eyes. Marsha was on one side of the bed, Rebecca on the other, staring down at him with worried, fearful looks. Laura stood weeping at the foot of the bed, her head cradled on Mrs. Burton's shoulder.

He felt coldly unemotional towards all of them. He was drained, exhausted, uncaring whether he lived or died. Perhaps death would be for the best, he thought. No need to recuperate, no need to ponder his dilemma further. And what were the consequences if he died? Laura and Rebecca were both young and would find other loves. Mrs. Burton would be sorry but might even be relieved. His mother? She would suffer the most. Without her husband and without her only child, she would be bereft of any anticipation of joy. Shattered, she might fall into the clutches of Uncle Avram. That alone persuaded Ephraim that he had to stay alive.

He closed his eyes, blotting out his visitors, and soon dozed off. Although the golden haze did not appear, he sensed the presence of Elijah and Alex and forestalled their appearance.

"Eliyahu, Alex, I know the arguments. Please, no more. I'll decide and my decision will be final."

But how to decide. The arguments on either side were equally compelling. Yet, as always, he leaned towards Laura. There was a bond between them that should have eclipsed Elijah's position. Then why do I equivocate?

Ephraim asked himself. Why am I even tempted to consider another option? Elijah's argument was that Ephraim's faith faltered at times and Rebecca would provide him with the strength needed. But there was no doubting Laura's sincerity — she would be a real support to him and fulfill the obligations and duties of a rabbi's wife.

He could understand why Elijah was constantly promoting Rebecca but the Prophet also condemned Laura as a Midianite. Yet it wasn't unknown for Israelites to marry Midianites. In a flash of memory, Ephraim recalled a biblical icon who had married a Midianite and who remained his only wife during their long life together. If only Ephraim could consult with him as a final piece of advice with which to make his decision.

A desert stretched all around him, the rocky, sandy soil radiating shimmers of heat from the overhead sun. Here and there outcrops of rock, sedge grass and the occasional tree broke up the vast expanse of wasteland. In the distance, a range of mountains stood out against the cloudless sky.

To the east, he saw something green poking through the heat haze. A forest of palms surrounding a series of interconnecting pools of water greeted him as he made his way to the sighting, hoping it wasn't just a mirage. In the shade of the palms, the heat abated somewhat. With cupped hands, he drank from a pool and found the water surprisingly cool. Refreshed, he explored the oasis and soon discovered he was all alone. Where was the man he had come to consult?

He heard them coming before he saw them — a muffled roar slightly louder than the hot breezes that blew through the oasis. In the west, filling the horizon, a cloud of dust rose above the shimmers. Out of the dust, a multitude of moving dots appeared. Soon he could hear the bawling of cattle, the cries and calls of people, and the tread of tens of thousands of feet. In awe, he realized he was witnessing the nomadic wandering of his people after the Exodus.

A group of horsemen approached the oasis but pulled up abruptly when they saw Ephraim at the edge of the palm forest. The horsemen were all bearded and wore leather helmets and tunics. Some were armed with short bronze swords, others with bows and quivers of arrows, and some with wooden battle clubs. Two of the riders trained their bows on him. They all looked around suspiciously.

The leader of the pack gave a sharp command and several horsemen galloped off. Ephraim could hear them trotting through the oasis. They soon reappeared and reported to the leader.

They moved closer and fanned out to form a semi-circle around Ephraim. The leader slid off his saddle and approached Ephraim, his sword levelled.

"Shalom Aleichem," Ephraim said.

"Aleichem Shalom," the leader replied but without much warmth. "You are alone. You wear strange raiment. Who are you? Whence come you? What do you here?"

"I come from a foreign land, a long distance away. I wish to speak with Moses."

The leader narrowed his eyes, clearly suspicious of Ephraim. "How come you here?" he asked belligerently, raising his sword until its point was inches away from Ephraim's throat. "You have no mount. Your feet are bare, pale and unmarked by sand and stone. There is no sign that others brought you here."

"I need neither mount nor feet nor others," Ephraim replied and realized how incredible he must sound. "It is important that I meet with Moses."

The man questioning him, backed away and sheathed his sword in the thong around his waist. He was tall, with a slim, heavily tanned face, a flattened nose and a beard more like a few days stubble. He continued to stare at Ephraim, his brow furrowed, his eyes narrowed in apprehension and concern. Clearly, there was a debate going on in his mind.

Ephraim held out his arms. "Hear, O Israel, the Lord is our God, the Lord is One," he exclaimed loudly so all could hear.

At this, the leader prostrated himself in front of Ephraim and the others leapt off their saddles and kneeled.

"Forgive your servant Joshua, Angel of God. I shall do as you wish."

Ephraim was on the verge of protesting that he wasn't an angel but quickly understood how he must appear, alone in the middle of a desert. To these people, imbued with the miracles they had witnessed in the departure from Egypt and their wanderings in the desert, there could be no other explanation for his presence. As an angel, he would have easy access to Moses. He decided to play the part.

"Arise Joshua of the tribe of Ephraim and men of Israel," he called out as grandly as he could.

Joshua and his men gathered respectfully around Ephraim, each in turn touching him.

"Heavenly One, will you return with us to the main body of our people? They are yet a distance away."

Ephraim preferred the relative coolness of the oasis to a hot, dusty ride through the desert.

"Nay," he said. "I shall wait here."

"Until we return then," Joshua said backing away and bowing. The horsemen galloped away.

Ephraim returned to the shelter of the palms and lay down at the edge of a pool. He looked up at the canopy of leaves, stretched out like wings, their fronds fluttering in the desert wind that wafted over them. This is like heaven, he thought.

"Perhaps I've died and have indeed become an angel," he said aloud.

"Dearest, you're not dead and you're going to live," said a female voice that sounded like his mother.

"Don't worry, he's delirious again." He recognized Cindy's voice.

"Can't something be done?" He heard Laura ask.

His mother and Laura were together — surely a good sign.

"We're doing everything we can," Cindy replied. "The antibiotics will soon get rid of the fever and that should end the delirium."

He dozed off again and found himself back at the oasis. The noise of the approaching multitude was unmistakably clear and close. He strode to the edge of the forest and watched in awe as a vast army of people and animals converged on the oasis and the promise of water. Horsemen blowing on shofars signalled their tribes to follow them to their appointed places at the campsite.

A man on a richly caparisoned camel rode rapidly towards Ephraim. The camel crouched, the man slid off, and bowing, greeted Ephraim: "Exalted One, you have called your servant Moses, and he is here. What do you wish of me? If you are the Angel of Death, I am not ready. There is yet much to be done. The Lord has placed a heavy burden on me, leading these fractious tribes to the Promised Land."

Moses was a large, well-built man, dressed in a white tunic under a flaxen cloak. Leather sandals bound with strips of linen covered his feet. Sharp piercing eyes, a broad nose, and high forehead were framed by a greying beard. His full head of hair was partly covered by a leather headdress,

Ephraim, confronted with the leader of the people of Israel, felt compelled to bow and hoped this would not blow his cover as an angel.

" Moses, leader of the children of Israel, I am not the Angel of Death. I have been sent on another matter. Our discussion can wait until after you have settled the people and refreshed yourself."

Ephraim could see that Moses was surprised. When does an angel of God put off his business to accommodate mundane tasks? But Ephraim wanted to wait until Moses was relaxed and perhaps his wife would be about.

The sound became deafening as the Israelites set up thousands of tents, shouting instructions to each other and to the children, and herding the bawling, bleating herds to the pools. Wooden buckets and goatskin gourds were filled with water and taken back to the tents which were spread in the desert and encircled the oasis.

Daylight soon failed and the night was lit with thousands of torches and cooking fires. A steady hum of voices and occasional singing could be heard.

A few tents were set up within the oasis. He recognized Aaron in front of one. He was older now, his beard grey, his hair thinning. A short distance away, a haughty looking woman, bare head raised imperiously, sharply supervised the work of servants and slaves setting up her tent. She was clearly not Moses' wife as his tent was being erected at the very centre of the oasis. Ephraim guessed she was Miriam, Moses' sister.

Moses' tent was rich in comparison to the others. It was covered in fine kid hides draped over a wooden structure that provided ample space inside. The sandy floor of the tent was covered with elegant rugs. A cooking fire outside the tent roasted a skinned lamb secured on a spit. Servants placed a wooden Egyptian chair outside the entrance to the tent and stuffed pillows beside it.

Moses arrived on foot and settled heavily on the chair. A woman brought him a bowl of water which he drank from and offered the rest to her. The woman settled on the cushions beside him. This was his wife, Zipporah, Ephraim concluded.

Moses wife called out softly and a servant brought another bowl of water and placed it at Moses' feet. His wife stripped off his sandals and washed his feet. Moses crinkled his toes appreciatively and ran his fingers affectionately through his wife's hair.

Ephraim waited until they had eaten and were sitting back enjoying the cool air. Several torches on poles illuminated the area in front of the tent. Both rose and bowed as Ephraim approached. Moses' wife left them and entered the tent but Ephraim could see she was just inside within earshot. Ephraim motioned Moses to be seated.

"Now, Exalted One, what wish you of me?"

"Leader of Israel," replied Ephraim, "I wish to discuss Zipporah, your wife."

Moses rose precipitously from his chair, clearly upset. "Do not harm Zipporah," he pleaded. "I have great affection for her. She is my comfort, my support, my confidante. I cannot fulfill the mission the Almighty has burdened me with unless she is by my side."

Ephraim, taken aback by the heat of Moses' protest, held out his arms placatingly.

"Great leader, I mean her no harm. Zipporah is a Midianite, a daughter of a priest of Midian. How has she adapted to the laws of Israel and the worship of our one true God?"

Moses shook his head in anger. "Aaron and Miriam mutter against her and have roused many Israelites to question her. But Zipporah is faultless and blameless. She has forsworn the gods of her father Jethro and is more steadfast in the observance of our law than many of those who rail against her. She has behaved with unquestioning loyalty to me since the time I delivered her from the rude shepherds who assaulted her."

Ephraim was satisfied with the answer and wondered how he could break off the contact. It struck him as ironic that three thousand years later he was having the same problem with family as Moses.

"It angers me," Moses continued, "that despite the many times she has saved my life, the people have the temerity to speak out against her, especially my brother and sister."

In his frustration Moses had stood up and strode up and down in front of the tent.

"When Jethro learned that I was not worshipping his gods, he threw me into a dungeon and left me to starve. Zipporah fed me secretly, at great risk to herself, until Jethro relented." Here Moses paused and laughed. "I shall hold in memory the look on his face when he opened the dungeon, expecting to find a desiccated corpse.

"Another time, when we were on our way into Egypt to free our people, we stopped at an inn for the night. We became aware that some of our followers were planning to kill our son Gershom because he was not circumcised. I confronted them and was prepared to die to save my son. With a sharp flint, Zipporah circumcised Gershom and as we prepared to engage in battle, presented the child for all to see. This immediately pacified the conspirators. Thus has my Zipporah demonstrated her loyalty and affection. I will not give her up, no matter how the people grumble."

Moses sat down and Ephraim took the opportunity to end the discussion.

"Be assured, Great Leader, that no harm will come to her. You have answered my query. Shalom Aleichem."

Ephraim bowed and walked away. He sat against a palm tree at the edge of the desert. There was no moon but the sky was alive with the sparkle of myriads of stars. The mass of humanity spread out around him was largely silent. A few cooking fires and torches here and there pierced the darkness. He closed his eyes and slept.

He awoke, back in his hospital bed. Pale sunlight filtered through the Venetian slats.

"Freml, how do you feel?" His mother leaned over and felt his forehead. "Your fever's gone. You were quite delirious again and were talking wildly. Something about an oasis — your nurse says all your dreams are about water — and you mentioned a woman's name, Zipporah. I thought you had another girlfriend but Laura reminded me it was Moses' wife. We've been here all night."

He raised his head. Laura was fast asleep in a lounge chair beside his bed, her head resting on an arm. After his conversation with Moses, he had put all doubts to rest. A flood of affection flowed through him, filling his eyes with tears.

"I'm feeling much better," he said.

"Sweetheart, I've talked things over with Laura during this long night. I'm convinced we aggravated your illness by bringing so much family pressure to bear. If you want to marry her, that's fine with me. Laura's a fine girl and very unselfish. She's helped me tremendously during the last few weeks. Standing in at the store so I could visit you. Ignoring my hostile attitude and treating me always with respect and affection. Her mother is the same type. I was obviously unfriendly when we met but she wished me well and is eager for your recovery. What can I say? I'm sorry I caused you both such distress. I called

Avram and Gertie this morning and told them that's it. Either they welcome Laura into the family or stay away from us."

Ephraim grasped his mother's hand and kissed it. "I know you'll be happy with us. Others will moan and groan but as long as our mothers are on board, the rest don't matter. Even Moses had to put up with criticism about Zipporah but he stuck to his guns and wouldn't give her up."

He saw his mother looking strangely at him. "It's in the Torah, Ma," he said smiling.

END

GLOSSARY OF
Jewish Terms

Beit Din	Rabbinical Courts
Chasidim	Members of a fundamental religious cult
Eliyahu	Elijah
Eliyahu Hanavi	Elijah the Prophet
Gefilte fish	Ground fish
Ger Tzedek	A convert to Judaism
Goy	Non-Jewish person
Kippa	Skullcap
Knishes	Potato buns
L'chaim	Cheers! Literally: to life
Lemele	Awkward man with poor social skills
Lokshin Kugel	Noodle cake
Lox	Smoked Salmon
Maariv	Evening service
Mazeltov	Congratulations
Mincha	Afternoon service
Minyin	Quorum of ten required for public prayer
Mishuga	Crazy
Rebbetsyn	Rabbi's wife

Rosh Hashanah	Jewish New Year, also referred to as The High Holidays
Schnapps	Alcoholic drink
Shabbat	The Sabbath, Saturday
Shabbat Shalom	Sabbath greeting
Shalom Aleichem	Greetings. Literally: Peace unto you
Shiksa	Gentile woman
Shiva	Mourning the death of immediate family members
Shlob	Slob
Shofar	Ram's horn used as bugle
Shul	Synagogue
Siddur	Traditional prayer book
Simcha	Happiness, joy
Talmud	Ancient texts of rabbinical analysis and debate re: The Old Testament
Torah	A sacred scroll containing the five books of Moses
Vai	Expression of pain or distress
Verenikes	Similar to perogies
Yom Kippur	Tenth day of New Year, holiest day in Jewish calendar

About the Author

With degrees in both Economics and English Literature, Sam Goldenberg enjoyed a business career on both sides of the Atlantic before taking up writing. His first book, *Dawn, the Planet* was published by Paradise Publishers in 2012. In writing *Ephraim-A Rabbi Strays...* Sam leaned heavily on his own personal experience in loving and marrying a non-Jewish woman. He and his wife, Rosemarie, live in Oakville, Ontario. They have been married more than fifty years.

Acknowledgements

I wish to thank Rachael Preston (Sheridan College) and Richard Scrimger (Humber School Of Writers) for teaching me the essential basics of creative writing. Whatever craft I have, I owe to them.

CPSIA information can be obtained at www.ICGtesting.com
Printed in the USA
LVOW13*0000280614

392155LV00002B/2/P